KUSHTAKA

DAVID PIERDOMENICO

Publisher's Note:
The following is a work of fiction. While some places
and references are inspired by a mixture of truth and
myth, all characters and events are fictitious or used
fictitiously. That said, the dark arts are nothing to
tamper with and the "ancient" book referenced in this
novel should not be sought out.

This is the First Edition Printing by DAP Publishing

DaveTheAuthor.com
@DaveTheAuthor

Printed in the U.S.A.

The enemy of my enemy is my friend...

...but these friendships are toxic and rarely last.

PROLOGUE

The flashing red and blue lights almost pulled little Mark into a trance. He had seen police cars on TV and sometimes while driving with Mommy or Daddy. But he never saw one in real life with its lights on, especially in front of his own house. It wasn't the only strange car in front of his house. There was an ambulance too, but he found the police car much more interesting.

Only minutes earlier Mommy had caught little Mark sneaking down the stairs. With tears in her eyes she had said, "Go on back to your room honey. It's okay." He knew that she and Daddy must have been fighting again. That was happening a lot lately. As he walked back to his room little Mark marveled at his own cleverness. Mommy had told him to go back to his room, but she didn't say anything about going back to bed. As soon as he was back in his room, he was standing on his stool and looking out his window at the front lawn.

Two policemen stood on the porch and talked to Mommy. Two other men carried Daddy out on top of this big wooden thing that looked like a surf board. Little Mark was intrigued as he noticed that Daddy's arms and legs were strapped down. He tried to pull them off, but they must have been really tight. For some reason, this did not surprise little Mark at all.

1

Daddy *had* been acting really weird lately. He and Mommy would fight, and Mommy would cry. She tried to keep little Mark from seeing, and like a good little six year old boy, he pretended he didn't.

As little Mark took a closer look, he saw some of the neighbors come out onto their porches. He wondered if any of them knew what was going on. Or maybe this whole thing was just one big secret among the grownups. Daddy started yelling something. Little Mark couldn't hear it very well and it was a hard word to understand. It almost sounded like he was saying, "belly" or "liar". But why would Daddy shout that?

The men put Daddy in the ambulance and drove away. The policemen nodded to Mommy and got back into their car too. Little Mark jumped back into bed and pretended to be sleeping the whole entire time. He had no brothers or sisters, so there was no one he could talk to about Mommy and Daddy's problems.

Later, Mommy told him that Daddy just needed a little help and he'd be okay. She said, "Sometimes grownups need a little help too." She told him that Daddy was going to a special hospital; a place that could help people when they were confused. He thought that it would all go back to normal soon. A week later, Mommy came to little Mark in tears again. This time she didn't even try to hide it. She told little Mark that Daddy had killed himself in the hospital. Life would never be the same again.

ONE

Mark was startled awake by the sounds of his mother crying. He wiped the sweat from his forehead and was surprised, considering how cold it was. What surprised him even more was that he had not thought about that day in years. As he drowsily sat up, he glanced over at his alarm clock. Not even six, but his alarm on his phone was about to go off. *Damn this new start time*, he thought to himself. He hadn't been getting up this early since college.

As he got up, he looked out the window at the vast and beautiful expanse of the Alaskan wilderness. He lived in a small cabin deep in the woods. From his window, he could see nothing but nature for miles. There wasn't much to be happy about in recent times, but even Mark had to admit that the morning view was nothing short of beautiful. As he stepped into the bathroom to shower, he took a good look at his reflection in the mirror, wondering whether or not to shave that day. It had been over 2 weeks since he had. As he had decided each and every previous morning, he figured, "Why bother?"

Mark had been living in Juneau now for six months. This proved long enough to get into the groove of his new life and *almost* forget about his old one. He took pleasure in the simple things: his scenic drive to work every morning and the simplicity of loading trucks with timber and watching them drive off. He arrived at work a few minutes early, enjoyed a cup of coffee and was clocked in and loading trucks before seven.

"Hey Taylor! Boss wants to see you in the office!" Mark heard these words, but didn't quite comprehend them. At the time, he was caught up with spacing out, as often happened. "Taylor!" the voice called once again. This time Mark noticed and realized that he was being called. He gave a quick nod, finished loading the truck he was on, and hurried over to the office.

Barry was a tall and stocky man, with light brown hair and a matching beard. To go with his look, he also wore nothing but jeans and flannel shirts. No one really knew if he was trying to look like a clichéd lumberjack or if it was just coincidence. Fitting the stereotype his look portrayed, he was a man of little words and meant everything he said. He was blunt, honest, stern, but also fair. As long as his guys did their job, they had no problems with him.

As Mark walked into his noticeably bare office, he wondered why he had been called. Barry had a reputation for only calling in workers to offer them a promotion or fire them. Mark took his chances and sat down in front of Barry's desk.

"You wanted to see me?" inquired Mark.

"Yeah, thanks for coming by," responded Barry in a deep, masculine voice that fit his appearance. He continued on, "How do you feel about management?"

"Management, wow. Um...I hadn't really thought about it to be honest."

"There's gonna be an Assistant Supervisor position

opening up to oversee loading and shipping."

"What about Tim? Isn't that his job?"

"I haven't announced it yet, but Tim just gave me his notice yesterday. Said he's moving back to Portland. Something about his dad's sick or something. I figured he would want to tell the guys himself, seeing as how it's kind of personal."

"If I may ask, why me? I've only been here since October. There's at least five other guys with more experience."

"That's true. But not all of them bust their ass every day without a single complaint or reported problem. You're by far the most reliable worker I've got out there."

"Thanks."

"Tell you what; don't give me an answer now. I want you to think about it. Give yourself a few days, see if it's right for you and get back to me, all right?"

"Sure."

Mark stood up and shook Barry's hand. Upon doing so, he was reminded that this man had spent his entire life working physical labor. His grip felt like a vice. Mark smiled and exited the office, still taking in this unexpected offer. The whole point of moving out here was to leave everything behind and stay below the radar. If he took this new position, he'd be overseeing at least forty people. Mark had reminded himself to get a job, any job, and come in every day and just work. Ironically this had gotten him attention.

It's not that he couldn't use the pay raise this would undoubtedly bring. It wasn't even that he feared resentment from his coworkers with more seniority. Honestly, Mark feared going down his old path again.

He had been good since moving here, but still didn't fully trust himself with any kind of authority. Even overseeing trees being cut down and put on trucks was too close a step towards his old life; one that he had worked hard to erase.

The rest of the day seemed to drag on. Mark found that spacing out from time to time helped with the monotonous tasks. He had a few run-ins with Tim, but felt awkward bringing anything up to him. Mark wasn't even sure that Tim was aware that he knew about his situation. As he loaded the last truck, he shut the sliding door hard and loud. Slamming it shut always felt satisfying after a long and exhausting day.

Less than an hour after clocking out, Mark was already quaffing down his first beer at McHenry's. Upon first moving to Alaska, Mark had been fairly surprised to learn that even Juneau had Irish pubs. Most of their clientele weren't exactly Alaskan natives. Jimmy, the bar's owner, made Mark laugh when he admitted that he only chose the name because it sounded Irish. McHenry's was a working class bar that catered to people that had moved to the area for a host of different reasons.

Most of Mark's coworkers could be found there every night. The fact that today was Monday only meant it would be mildly crowded. McHenry's offered Mark and his peers a little taste of their old lives. They affectionately referred to themselves as "the exiles" since most of them had either been kicked out, or forced to leave wherever they came from. Mark was no different. To his drinking buddies, he was Mark Taylor, disbarred lawyer from Philadelphia. *If only they knew the truth*, he wondered.

As he sat in awkward silence, waiting for his coworkers to show up, he made small talk with Caitlin while she tended bar. Twenty-three years old, long brown hair and bright blue eyes, there was no denying Caitlin's attractiveness. Being recently divorced, Mark found it hard to keep his eyes off her. Most of the guys there felt the same way, but look was all they ever did. Caitlin was Jimmy's oldest daughter and due to his affinity for hunting and his vast rifle collection, most of them kept their distance. Mark had remembered hearing that she helped her dad take care of her three younger siblings. He felt bad that he couldn't remember their names or ages, knowing that she had told him at some point.

"How are the kids?" inquired Mark.

"They're doing good. They're a pain in the ass, but they keep me busy," laughed Caitlin.

Mark felt relieved when he saw Tim and the other guys walk in. He nodded to them and they sat around him. Within twenty minutes, the night became loud and jovial. Tim took this opportunity to make his announcement that he would be leaving in a few weeks. Among the crowd was a face Mark didn't recognize. The guy looked straight out of high school and was short, but buff. It took him a moment, but then he did remember seeing him at work the previous week. The guys must have been "inducting" him tonight at McHenry's. He introduced himself as Paul. Like all the others, Paul had been somebody somewhere else.

"Almost went to law school back in Philly, but money got in the way," explained Paul.

"Hey, Mark's from there too," remarked one of them.

"No way, where?" asked Paul, his attention on Mark.

"I lived in the suburbs."

"Which one?"

"Um...Delaware County."

The answer seemed to satisfy Paul enough to resume conversation with someone else. He had come dangerously close to stumping Mark. He had been so paranoid of his new friends looking him up, that he made up a fake backstory when he first arrived. He returned to his drink and managed to enjoy the rest of the night. When Caitlin started kicking out rowdy drunks, Mark took it as his cue to leave. She may have been young, but Caitlin had inherited a lot from her bold and borderline psychotic father.

As he went into the parking lot, he was held up by Tim. They spoke for a few minutes about Mark taking over for Tim when he left. Mark knew that he would probably accept, since the money certainly didn't hurt. What bothered him the most was the realization that this is what his life had become. A year earlier, he was on top the world and set for the rest of his life. He knew deep down that he didn't have anyone to blame but himself. But all that did was make him feel worse.

He crawled into bed, with this thought stuck in his mind. That and regret for drinking so much on a work night. He heard that this state had high rates of alcoholism and depression. He worried the depression would get him due to his predicament. Who knew it would probably be both? He glanced at the clock and realized it was past midnight. For a brief moment, he thought he heard scratching from outside his window. *Probably just the beer*, he figured. As his mind slowly calmed down, he drifted off to sleep.

TWO

Governor Joe Thomas stood at his podium addressing the press and attempting not to squint at the dozens of camera flashes in his face. He spoke in his usual deep voice and Buffalo accent, "It's no secret that our state was suffering from this vacancy in my cabinet. But we've just successfully elected and approved the new Department Head of Audits and Control. Things will no doubt, work much smoother from now on. He's an old friend and it gives me great pleasure to introduce you to our New York State Comptroller, Mark Pallano."

Right on cue, Mark walked out and greeted the crowd. He shook hands with Joe and gave a sincere smile. He owed this man everything. If it wasn't for his old law school classmate, he'd still be a corporate accountant in a failing firm. He took the podium and addressed the press. "Well thanks for the no pressure Joe." The crowd gave an obligatory chuckle. He continued, "I certainly have my work cut out for me. But I'm looking forward to serving the great people of this state." In his Armani suit and $200 haircut, he knew he was set for life.

The loud obnoxious alarm robbed Mark of any last minute rest. As he groggily wiped his eyes, he caught the last few glimpses of his dream. He couldn't quite remember the whole thing, but something told him that he didn't want to. He got up, ate a few pieces of buttered toast and made his way out the door.

As he walked to his truck, he noticed scratches on the wall of his wooden cabin, just underneath his bedroom window. The sun was still not quite up, but the scratches were pronounced enough to notice. Mark walked over to take a closer look. They were at least a few inches long. He took a picture with his phone and made a mental note to stop by the hardware store later. And another note to keep an eye out for whatever the hell was living in the woods behind the backyard. Given his lack of knowledge about this location, it could have been anything.

Work went by extra slow today. The hangover certainly didn't help. Mark swore he was never going out on a Monday night ever again. He met up with Paul, since Barry had asked Mark to help train him. Neither one said it out loud, but Barry was testing Mark to see if he was management material. Mark reluctantly accepted the task with nothing more than a nod.

Four hours into their shift, it was almost lunch and Mark had to admit he was impressed. This was hardly the most complex job in the world, but Paul really seemed to know what he was doing from the get go. Mark was much more optimistic about overseeing workers if this is how easy it could be.

"So how long you been working here?" asked Paul, trying to make conversation. "Just about six months now," answered Mark, now on his guard to keep his secret.

"What kind of work did you do back in Philly?

Or…well, Delaware County right?"

"Yeah, I lived in Upper Darby," responded Mark, only knowing the name after quickly Googling "towns in Delaware County, PA" the night before. He continued on,

"I was a corporate accountant."

"That sounds…exciting," chuckled Paul.

"I sat at a desk for eight hours a day counting other people's money. The worst part was knowing just how much more they made than I did."

Mark surprised himself at how open he was being. Sure, he lied about where he was from, but before he got his comptroller dream job he was a miserable accountant. He missed Buffalo, but he definitely didn't miss that job. His wife at the time, Livia, always urged him to just quit. And he would always ask her to understand that it wasn't that simple.

He and Paul spent lunch and the rest of the afternoon getting to know each other. Paul seemed like a pretty good guy. At the very least, he was someone Mark could tolerate working with for hours at a time. A lot had sucked about this move, but he was starting to enjoy working outdoors. Working outside and seeing the vast expanse of forest, constantly reminded him of how imprisoned he always felt at his desk back in New York.

After clocking out, Mark drove into town looking for a hardware shop. He took a route he didn't normally take and quickly found himself lost. He wondered how a town so small could have so many twists and turns. Still, there was something serene to this place. At least there had been when he first moved there. He had to admit that this place was starting to seem shitty and he understood what the lifers here meant when they spoke so contemptuously about their hometown. Now he figured he had been here a few months and the honeymoon was over.

Mark had gotten so caught up with his thoughts that he almost forgot what he was looking for and drove right past a hardware store generically called, "Tools & More". He quickly did a "U" turn and drove into the parking lot. This place hardly seemed like a Home Depot in scale, but its name was just cheesy enough to be a big chain.

He walked into the small, but quaint shop and was greeted by a tall man with a thinning ponytail and decorative earrings, but countered with a vest, glasses and a name tag that read, "Hi, my name is Ethan". Ethan nodded to Mark and queried, "Good evening sir, how may I help you?" This left Mark no opportunity to pretend like he was just looking or killing time, while awkwardly trying to find his item without asking for help. "I was looking for something to fill in scratches on wood," Mark obligatorily replied.

"Floor, table or furniture?"

"Outside wall actually. I'm in a cabin."

"Oh, up by the lake?"

"Yeah."

"It must be beautiful up there."

"Uh…yeah it is. Anyway I took a picture on my phone."

Mark pulled up the picture on his phone and handed it over to Ethan. Mark detected a slight hint of surprise and even anxiety when Ethan first saw the picture, but he was quick to put a smile back on his face; a sign of a true expert in customer service. "I was hoping you guys had some sort of paste or putty or something to fill it in with," explained Mark. He continued, "I feel like you're probably more familiar with this area than me, so I gotta ask. What kind of animal could have done that?" Ethan handed Mark his phone back and shook his head.

"Well the truth is it could be anything. They are deep so it could be a bear or something as small as an otter."

"An otter could have done that?"

"You'd be surprised at how strong they are."

Mark and Ethan conversed for about another twenty minutes. Mostly just small talk pleasantries followed by the business at hand. Ethan recommended this odd looking paste that he had used before, along with a stain that would match the original color of the wood. Despite being reluctant to make any new friends, Mark had enjoyed Ethan's company. He doubted he would interact with him very often, but this served as a small glimmer of hope that life could be normal again. After remembering his awful hangover earlier that day, Mark decided to skip McHenry's and head straight home.

Mark ate a quick dinner and got to bed early to make up for the night before. Usually he tossed and turned, but tonight he was downright exhausted. As he began to fall asleep, he could have sworn he heard the scratching again. He hadn't gotten the chance to fix it up tonight and figured he would just fix up the new ones tomorrow too.

THREE

Little Mark wandered from his room into the hallway. The banging of his closet door woke him up for the third time this week. He kept telling Mommy and Daddy that he was scared, but no one ever believed a kid. They would just say, "Go back to sleep honey," or "You're just imagining things." But little Mark knew what he heard.

He crept down the stairs and could hear Mommy and Daddy yelling from the kitchen. They were always arguing. Something about Daddy was spending too much time in his office. Little Mark always wondered what he did in there, since he was never allowed in. But whatever it was, Mommy didn't seem to like it. Little Mark didn't understand what the big deal was. Once when Daddy was going into the office, he saw inside for a second. It was nothing but these weird red and black candles on the floor.

"Just please, come with us to church this week," Mommy pleaded.

"Why, so you don't have to lie to the neighbors again? Tell them the truth. I'm conducting research."

"How the hell am I supposed to explain what you do? It's bad enough to even have that shit in our house, but what am I supposed to think when you go in there and don't come out for hours?!"

KUSHTAKA

Mark woke up feeling much better and well rested than yesterday. He took it as a good sign. The morning went pretty well. He seemed to be in a good mood and was working by himself most of the morning. He enjoyed Paul's company, but sometimes just preferred to be alone. Barry had taken a rare step out of his office, since a few guys had called out today. Paul had gone with him and a few others up into the denser part of the woods to prep trees to be cut.

It was almost lunchtime when the entire lumber mill, and probably the town heard it. Mark was just finishing up one truck and closing up the back of it when it stopped him dead in his tracks. A piercingly loud, terrified and agonizing scream came from the trees. Every worker dropped whatever they were doing, including heavy timber, and ran towards the sound. Mark raced up the hill and into the woods. After the initial scream, additional groans and cries echoed in a grotesque harmony.

As they got closer, a voice called out, "It's Barry! He's pretty bad!" Mark instantly recognized it to be Paul and feared for the worst. When he and about ten others reached Paul they looked down at Barry and their worst fears were realized. There was Barry leaned up against the tree. His right leg was missing below the knee and three gaping scratches protruded across his chest. Blood oozed out of his wounds and stained the ground around him. Barry himself was breathing in short, shallow breaths and smeared vomit was left on his shoulder and around his mouth.

No one there was a doctor, but it was clear that Barry had gone into shock and needed medical attention immediately. Paul had already removed his belt and tied it tightly around Barry's leg as a makeshift tourniquet. Mark had a million questions for Paul, as did everyone else, but now wasn't the time for it. They took some tarp and fashioned it into a makeshift stretcher and loaded Barry into the back of Mark's truck since it was parked closest.

The entire time they moved him, Barry kept repeating, "Tim, I need those reports Tim. Make sure I have them. We gotta stay under budget Tim." No doubt the trauma had left him delirious and for some reason financial reports really seemed to be in the back of Barry's mind. Most of the guys, deep down, worried this meant possible layoffs, but Barry's well-being was the more immediate concern.

Mark and Paul agreed to drive Barry to the hospital. Tim, as Assistant Supervisor, would need to stay behind and oversee the work crews. Mark didn't imagine much would get done or if anything could get done, pending the inevitable OSHA investigation. Paul sat in the back of the truck tending to Barry while Mark drove as fast as he could. The nearest hospital was twenty miles away and he floored the gas pedal the entire way, still being careful not to fling Barry and Paul off the back.

As the truck pulled into the ambulance bay, Mark pounded the horn again and again. A group of doctors and nurses sprinted out and immediately took to the ailing Barry. By now, he was unconscious and Mark honestly thought he might be dead. Within seconds, they had Barry on a stretcher and inside. An orderly instructed Mark to park in the garage and come in through the ER entrance. Mark obliged, while Paul ran in to stay with Barry.

KUSHTAKA

After leaving his car and paying a ridiculous amount for temporary parking, Mark made his way into the ER. He was still trying to make sense of what had just happened. As he entered the waiting room, he found Paul sitting and staring off into space. When he saw Mark and his sense of urgency, he spoke first: "It's not good. Doctor said they'll do the best they can. I read between the lines."

"What the hell happened out there?" asked Mark as he exhaled deeply.

"We were up there marking trees for the next crew to come in. I heard the scream, ran over and saw…that!"

"Wait, you didn't actually see it happen?"

"No, my back was turned to him."

"How? You're telling me you turned around and he was…in pieces and the animal just disappeared?!"

"I don't know! Barry had a can of paint, I had mine. We were joking. Then he went to one tree, I went to another. We were about thirty feet apart. Everything was fine! I heard him scream, just like you guys did. How the hell could I have not seen what did it?!"

Mark put a reassuring hand on Paul's shoulder. Initially, he had been slightly suspicious of the circumstances. The fact that Paul was there, but claimed to see nothing definitely raised eyebrows. Mark went from interrogating Paul to simply trying to comfort him. The fear in his voice, the tears forming in his eyes seemed pretty genuine. Mark's suspicions weren't entirely alleviated, but were certainly toned down.

For the next few hours, Mark and Paul sat in the waiting room killing time. They read magazines, watched the TV, made small talk and at times, sat in complete and awkward silence. Each time a door opened or someone dressed in scrubs walked by they anxiously looked up, hoping this was someone who had news for them. Though neither man would ever admit it, they wouldn't have minded if the news was Barry's death. At least knowing wasn't as bad as waiting in silent uncertainty.

Finally, a weathered looking doctor with blood stains on his scrubs walked over and seemed to be looking for someone. Mark took the initiative and walked right up.

"Were you the ones that came in with Barry Jenson?" asked the doctor.

"Yeah, how is he?" responded Mark.

"He's lost quite a bit of blood, but he's stable for now. Are either of you next of kin?"

"No, we just work with him," replied Mark, while Paul simply shook his head. Mark continued, "He has a brother up in Anchorage. I don't have his number, but I'm sure it's somewhere in his office. Was it in his phone?"

"His phone is in pieces with the rest of his clothing."

The doctor's professional wall fell and a look of utter disbelief remained. He slowly opened his mouth, stayed silent for a second then asked, "What the hell got ahold of him?" Mark and Paul were just as dumbfounded as this experienced Emergency Room Doctor. And that was not a comforting thought. Paul recanted everything the same way he had explained to Mark. He couldn't tell if this doctor believed him or not. All he knew was that something large and ferocious had attacked his friend who was now fighting for his life.

Despite not being family, the doctor allowed Mark and Paul into Barry's room for just a moment to see him. There was no way anyone could truly prepare for the sight they gazed upon. It was like ripping off a band aid, best done quickly and without hesitation. As they stepped in, the doctor reminded them that Barry was heavily sedated and was therefore not conscious. Mark had to admit he preferred it this way.

The wound on Barry's leg had been sewn up and the bleeding stopped. He was covered in bandages and hooked up to so many IVs and monitors that he didn't even seem human. Seeing all the wires in Barry reminded Mark of a science project he once did involving a potato and electricity. He and Paul were grateful that, at the very least, Barry's chest moved up and down ever so slightly.

At this point, neither Mark nor Paul had said much to each other. But both knew that they had had all they could take for the day and decided to drive back. They called the lumber mill to give everyone an update on Barry's condition. Mark dropped Paul off by his car and kept driving. He figured that technically he was supposed to check in or at least clock out, but after today, he didn't really care.

As he drove by McHenry's he stopped for a moment and debated whether or not to go in. He could certainly use a drink after today, but at the same time he was exhausted and didn't want to be bothered. As often happens in Alaska, alcohol won. He pulled into McHenry's promising himself he'd stay for less than an hour.

Jimmy himself was tending bar. Word spread fast in this town, as evidenced by the fact that Jimmy and all of his patrons were well aware of Barry's incident earlier in the day. When Mark first sat down he was bombarded with questions ranging from "Did you see what did it?" to the more concerned, "How's Barry doing?" After about an hour it calmed down and Mark got a chance to talk with Jimmy.

"That damn thing comes anywhere near this establishment, he'll meet my Winchester!" exclaimed Jimmy. Here he was on one of his rants...again. He continued on about his array of firearms and how each one would bring unimaginable carnage and despair upon any person or creature that attempted to break into his bar. Mark had learned whenever Jimmy got on his soapbox, the best thing to do was to nod and occasionally say, "I know man, I know."

Two hours into the night, Mark was half tuning Jimmy out and half enjoying his drink when Jimmy caught his attention again. "You still got that rifle I lent ya?" asked Jimmy. Mark felt embarrassed that he had forgotten about it till just now. Right around when he first moved out there, Jimmy and a few coworkers invited him out hunting. He hadn't caught anything, but it was a nice icebreaker for getting to know the townspeople.

"Yeah, I'm sorry. I meant to give it back to you sooner," replied Mark.

"Nah, that's all right. You hang on to it for now. World's getting crazier."

Mark finished his beer and gave Jimmy a generous tip. He went home and didn't realize until he was already in bed that he forgot to look at the scratches on the wall. It didn't matter. It could wait for morning. After about a half hour, Mark finally fell asleep.

FOUR

"Mark, you understand what I'm telling you?"
No answer.
"Mark?"

Mark's generic office phone suddenly felt quite heavy. The plastic hadn't increased in mass, but the news he was hearing from it was nothing short of devastating. Carl, his stockbroker in Manhattan, had just given Mark the news that a certain company's stock had just plummeted and the CEO declared bankruptcy. They had been successful in hiding how badly they were doing after the recession hit, but there was no denying it now. Normally Mark wouldn't have cared except for the small fact that half of his net worth was tied up in this company's stock.

"Yeah Carl, I understand."

"I'm sorry Mark. Wish I had better news. This place has been a madhouse all morning. Wasn't just this company either…"

"Carl, if it's all the same to you, I don't really give a shit about the other companies."

"Fair enough, sorry. Look, I gotta go. Lot more phone calls to make. Hang in there Mark, I'll be in touch."

Mark slammed down the phone without as much as a 'goodbye'. He wasn't mad at Carl so much as he was at the situation. He figured Carl knew that. To be honest, he didn't really care. How in the hell was he going to explain this to Livia? He had only occupied his comptroller post for three months and that was supposed to make things better. Their lives were supposed to be set from here on out.

His salary was generous, but they had become accustomed to a much higher standard of living. There was the six bedroom McMansion in Buffalo, the condo here in Albany, and Livia had taken off practicing cases for a year to co-author a law textbook. Sure, it was something interesting for her to do and would pay off in the end, but right now Mark was looking at about $900,000 of debt. He had invested everything he had in this company, hoping it would solve all his money problems. Like a wounded animal, Mark was desperate and willing to do anything.

A knock came at his office door, startling him out of his trance. "Come in," he called, curious who it could be. He didn't have any meetings scheduled for another two hours. In walked his lovely wife Livia with a take-out bag in her hand and wide smile on her face. "Hey honey, what are you doing here?" asked Mark trying to conceal his inner panic. Livia sat down and put the bag on his desk and replied, "I was in the area."

Livia had been with Mark since the beginning. They met at Cornell Law and instantly connected. Initially, it was her glistening blonde hair and bright blue eyes that caught Mark's attention. Their relationship and marriage was based on love, but also a respect for each other's careers. Mark was an up and coming legal accountant looking for his big break and

Livia worked her way up the criminal justice ladder wanting to settle for nothing less than the Supreme Court. They had decided to postpone having children, if ever having them, to see how far they could go. Mark was now comptroller of New York State and Livia had worked with the district attorneys of both Buffalo and New York City.

With their busy schedules, a moment to sit and enjoy lunch together was rare, so they both cherished it. Mark wasn't sure how much of his current emotion was held on his sleeve, but he tried his best to hide it. He didn't want to burden Livia with this knowledge, but that wasn't his primary reason. Making a few bad investments and betting so much on them had proven to be a foolish decision, and it made Mark question his competency as an accountant and even as a man. For the moment, he tried to just enjoy the sandwich Livia had brought him, having no idea how they'd pay for it.

The sound of his phone woke Mark up out of his sleep. He didn't mind so much, seeing as his alarm would have gone off in ten minutes anyway. By the time he was conscious enough to grab his phone and check it; a message was already left on it. It was Paul: "Hey Mark, listen, just heard from Barry's brother that he woke up and he's starting to do better. Just wanted to let you know. I know I'll see you at work soon but I figured…you know. Anyway, a few of us are going over to visit Barry in the hospital during lunch today. Thought maybe you'd wanna go. I'll see you shortly. Bye."

Mark chuckled slightly at the overall awkwardness of the message. He still didn't know Paul that well and never remembered giving him his number. *Must have gotten it from anyone else,* he figured. He quickly got up, showered and headed for work. He called Paul back on his way there and told him he would join them over lunch.

Tim was irritable all morning. Mark figured that now with Barry being injured, Tim would have to stay on indefinitely. He barked orders and even lost his temper with Paul when he didn't tie a knot properly the first time. Mark shrugged it off and kept his mouth shut. Tim was the very last thing on his mind at the moment.

The entire lumber mill was far behind after yesterday's accident. Mark and Paul went up to mark the trees that Barry was working on. Despite having a lot to potentially talk about, both men kept pretty quiet. Mark wasn't sure about Paul, but there was something unsettling about being up here. Whatever animal had mauled Barry so grotesquely hadn't been caught, let alone even identified. Neither he nor Paul would admit that they were absolutely terrified to be up here. Each twig snap and leaf crunch caused them to flinch.

Lunch couldn't come soon enough. When it did, Mark, Paul and several others headed off for the hospital to see Barry. They knew they'd only get a few minutes, but just seeing him alive and awake would make a world of difference. Barry's brother was there and greeted everyone and thanked them for coming. He then reminded them that Barry still needed his rest but would be pleased to see them.

Mark went in with Paul and both tried to contain their repulsion. Barry, while smiling at the sight of them, looked much worse than his smile suggested. His stub, where a leg once sat, was bandaged, along with his face and a long row of stitches stretched across his chest. He was also hooked up to an array of tubes and machines, each with their own unique rhythmic beeping.

"I look that bad huh?" laughed Barry. There was nothing to do but laugh and admit the truth. "Hey man, you're still breathing and that counts for a lot," remarked Paul. They talked for only a few minutes and Barry expressed his immense gratitude to both of them for getting him to the hospital in time. Normally, he was monotone and deadpan, but today he was downright emotional. It was strange to see, but Mark understood completely. As they were about to leave, Paul felt the urge to ask one more thing:

"Barry, what the hell did this? I know you need your rest and probably shouldn't be thinking about it. But I was right there. How the hell did I miss it?"

"Kid, don't even worry about it. I have no idea either. Came out of nowhere and whole thing is a blur to me. There was nothing you could do right then and there, except for get me here which you did. And I'll never forget that."

Paul smiled, satisfied with Barry's response, but equally disturbed that neither of them could determine what did this. The two of them headed out, nodded to other guys waiting to get a glimpse of Barry awake and optimistic, and headed back to work.

On the way back, Mark wasn't sure why, but he brought up the gaping scratches on his cabin. "Hey Paul, you ever know an animal to tear up the side of a house but not go for any food in the garbage can?"

"That's weird," replied Paul, the gears in his head now turning.

"I'll show you."

Mark, mindful of his driving, handed Paul his phone and told him where to pull up the pictures. Paul took a look at the first one. His eyes widened with shock. He swiped through the others and suddenly began to breathe heavier. He put the phone down and looked away. Mark was concerned by this reaction of his, especially since he thought he knew exactly what Paul was thinking.

"Those scratch marks are the same from Barry's wounds aren't they?" asked Mark.

"When did this happen?"

"Last couple days. Guy at the hardware store thought it might be a bear."

"No way in hell a bear attacked Barry that fast and just vanished into thin air!"

"What then?"

Paul merely shrugged his shoulders. Neither of them had any idea. They sat in silence for the remainder of the ride, as a feeling of dread began to set in. Mark wasn't sure what was going on, but somehow just knew that it was going to get worse before it got better. Unfortunately, that had always been the case for his entire life.

Mark kept to himself the rest of the day and raced to his truck after clocking out. He saw Paul at a distance and thought he might want to talk more about this connection between Barry and the scratches, but Mark wanted no part of that. He regretted even bringing it up. On some level he felt that giving it recognition made it worse. And so he was driving home while some guys were still making their way to the time clock.

Mark spent a quiet night in his cabin watching reruns on TV. It wasn't his normal forte, but he had enough for the last few days and he certainly wasn't going back to McHenry's *again* on a work night. *Shit,* he thought to himself upon realizing that he forgot again to take a look at the scratches on the wall. He looked at the time on his TV and it wasn't even nine yet. It was worth it, especially since he probably wouldn't feel like doing it tomorrow.

Armed with a flashlight, vinegar and his coat, Mark traipsed out into the darkness. He flicked on the flashlight and approached the wall. *How did it get this cold in just two hours?* He shined the light on it and lo and behold, the scratches were now deeper and more numerous. One had protruded so far in that it was about to poke through to the inside.

He opened up the bottle of vinegar and doused the entire area in it. He had heard somewhere that the pungent odor repelled animals. It was too dark and cold to bother with trying to patch it up. He'd put a reminder on his phone for the morning. He closed up the bottle and left it there, figuring that he'd use it again tomorrow, and prepared to walk back inside.

Just then, an unmistakable voice called out from the forest surrounding his house. It uttered only one word. "Mark!" it called with urgency. Mark's heart nearly jumped out of his throat. The fact that it startled him was only secondary in his terror. There was no denying who the voice belonged to. It was one he had not heard in many years. Immediately he recognized the voice as his father's.

It called out again, "Mark!" *You're just imagining this,* he told himself. *Dad's dead. He killed himself in a psych ward and at his funeral everyone told you how sorry they were.* Mark stood, frozen in his tracks. Finally, when it called his name a third time, he mustered the courage to move. He ran back into the cabin and slammed the door shut.

Immediately, he ran to his radio and put music on to drown out the sound. He wanted to look into the trees outside, but was too afraid to. The voice called him an additional ten times over the next half hour. In an attempt to rationalize this, Mark determined that either he was dreaming or his father's schizophrenia had passed onto him. He hoped that he was dreaming.

Just when Mark grew comfortable with a prolonged stint of silence, he heard another sound. It wasn't his dead father calling his name, but it was equally disturbing. An ear piercing, terrified scream echoed from the darkness. Most unsettling of all was that this voice sounded like it belonged to a child. Mark immediately sprang up and stood staring at the door as if some unseen evil was on the other side.

Following the scream, Mark stood still, hoping it was still in his imagination. For some instinctive reason, he ran for the closet where he kept the rifle loaned to him by Jimmy. As he picked it up, he wiped off a coat of dust and slung it by its strap over his shoulder. Just then it screamed again. He had no idea what was out there, if the rifle would work or if he was even experienced enough to be effective with it.

He burst out of his front door just when he heard the scream again. Like a hound following a scent, he followed the sound. He clicked on the flashlight and ran deep into the forest. The scream came again for a fourth time and he flinched as he stepped on a twig and thought something was behind him.

"Do you need help?! Where are you?!" he called into the vast nothingness that surrounded him. He felt that talking to it helped him forget just how frightened he really was. He continued on, routinely calling out, "Where are you?" It seemed useless. *Dammit, I always knew I'd go nuts like Dad did,* he thought to himself. It was a difficult idea to get out of his head. While he never talked about it, the memory of his father had always haunted him. It was as if that event had followed him his entire life.

Just then a few large branches snapped to Mark's left. He turned, and in the darkness, saw two bright red eyes glaring right at him. He jumped back three feet and nearly had a heart attack, right then and there. He dropped the flashlight and reached for the rifle when a feral roar came from the direction of the glowing eyes. It sounded like either a bear or something even larger. He fired a shot and the recoil pushed him back, causing him to drop the rifle as well.

Rather than stay and attempt to grab the rifle or flashlight again, Mark turned around and ran faster than he ever had in his life. Within seconds, he could see the light from inside his cabin to guide him. He sprinted through the yard and slammed the door shut behind him. Collapsing on the floor out of shock and exhaustion, Mark caught his breath. He barricaded the front door with a large chair and made for his bedroom, also putting a chair in front of the door.

Mark lay awake for hours, confused, terrified and feeling lucky to be alive. Whatever was out there had to be the same thing that attacked Barry. Mark hoped to god that the child screaming was also just a figment of his tormented psyche. By two or three in the morning (he wasn't really sure) Mark finally fell asleep. His dream however, gave him neither peace nor solace.

FIVE

Little Mark tiptoed across the carpet floor of the living room. He made it down the stairs without making a sound and Mommy and Daddy thought he was asleep. He would be soon, but right now he just wanted a peek. Nobody told kids anything and he knew he wasn't allowed in, but he just wanted to see what was there. He wasn't going to touch or play with anything in there.

As he approached the cracked door to Daddy's office, he smelled something funny. It was that weird smell he hated every time he and Mommy passed the candle store in the mall. He could hear Daddy talking in the room. He was saying something in a funny language. Little Mark couldn't understand a word of it. He would just get one little peek, then go right back up to his room and to bed. Mommy and Daddy would never even know.

He stepped over to an angle where he could see through the small crack in the door. There was Daddy, talking his strange words. He was reading from this big black book with gold pictures on the cover. It wasn't a book like Little Mark had ever seen. All around Daddy was a circle of lit candles. That explained the awful smell. Then little Mark stepped back in horror as he saw the book float in the air just above Daddy's hands.

Little Mark walked backwards and knocked into a lamp. It came down and the light bulb shattered with a crash. Daddy sprung up and came out of his room. When he saw Little Mark on the floor just outside, he was furious. Daddy slapped Little Mark across his face with his hand and shouted, "I told you never to come in here!!!" His voice even sounded different. Little Mark ran back upstairs and into his bed. In the morning Daddy didn't say anything about it, so little Mark decided it must have just been a dream.

As Mark drove into work the next morning, he tried to put the previous night behind him. While on his way, he would usually pass by McHenry's, and at this hour of the morning it was always dead quiet. Surely everyone that had been there the night before had gone home, or was sound asleep in their car in the parking lot.

Upon passing by the faux Irish establishment, Mark saw something he didn't expect. A large crowd had gathered in the parking lot. He spotted Paul and a few other guys from work. Mark then spotted five police cars and a dozen or so officers. There was even the local news van with the attractive redhead and her overeager cameraman. Something was going on and Mark clearly missed the memo.

He found an open spot down the street, parked his car and walked his way over to McHenry's. As he got closer, he made out Jimmy and Caitlin standing next to the reporter. Father and daughter were both in tears. Normally this overly masculine and self-proclaimed gun nut never showed a sliver of emotion. Now, here he was wiping fresh tears from his face and clearly embarrassed that he had them. Something wasn't right with the whole picture.

Paul spotted Mark and waved him over to him. "What the hell's going on Paul?" inquired Mark with sense of concern and urgency. Paul looked down and shook his head with empathy. He explained, "It's Kelly, Jimmy's youngest. She's missing. No one's seen her since last night." Right then it hit Mark like a punch in the stomach. Those screams he heard last night *were* real.

"Please, if anyone out there has her or any information, I beg you to come forward," pleaded Jimmy right into the news camera, "I'm not even angry, I just want my little girl back."

Jimmy broke down and Caitlin put her arm around him and walked him over to the curb to sit down. Police Captain Helmke stepped forward and cleared his throat loudly. "Listen up!" he called out to the crowd. He was a man deeply respected by the townspeople and this was a time of particular emergency, so everyone complied. With the crowd silent in seconds, Captain Helmke spoke again:

"I want us on the move within the hour. That gives us about thirty-eight minutes. We're gonna split up into groups and each take a general area to search. Most local businesses have agreed to open late today to help out with the search. Remember, the child was last seen only nine hours ago. Our best chances at finding her are in the next few hours!"

Mark intentionally didn't go with the group from the lumber mill. He had enough on his mind that he couldn't bother to humor them with small talk, or constantly reference Barry's situation and how this all might be related. Mark was afraid he already knew the answer to that question. In the crowd, he had spotted Ethan, the clerk from the hardware store and decided to go with him. Captain Helmke roughly divided up a ten mile radius into sections. Mark and Ethan were given the commercial center of town. Mark was relieved not to be scouring the woods as so many would be doing, but the thought of looking in dumpsters and finding Kelly would be unbearable.

"So how'd the wall repair go," asked Ethan as Mark drove his truck another lap around the supermarket, looking for anything out of the ordinary.

"To be honest, didn't even get to it."

"Hey, I know how that goes. If you need it, I could help."

"Thanks, I may take you up on that."

They spent the next hour driving around town, looking for any evidence or information they could find. Mark's stomach was in knots as he considered confessing what he heard the night before. Giving them a more specific place to look would certainly help, but then everyone would ask how he knew, or why he didn't say anything the night before. Of course then he'd also have to tell them about his dead dad calling his name out.

I can't tell. I wish I could help, but I can't, he told himself to try and justify his silence. He had worked too damn hard to build a new life for himself after Albany. Revealing this information would at best, label him a lunatic or at worst, he would be accused of kidnapping her. He sincerely meant no ill will towards poor little Kelly. He wanted her to be found safe and sound. But he had to protect himself first and foremost. This mentality had allowed him to survive as long as he did in his old life. Though it certainly didn't help him sleep at night.

"How long you been out here?" asked Ethan, trying to break the awkward silence.

"About six months now."

"Yeah, I had seen you around town. You work at the lumber mill right?"

Mark simply nodded, trying to multitask between this conversation, his driving and his guilt.

"Where from originally?" continued Ethan. *Damn, this guy's persistent.*

"Philadelphia. I was an accountant at a law firm. It's a long story, don't ask."

"Always is," chuckled Ethan.

"How about you?" asked Mark, turning the attention off of him.

"Born and raised right in Southeastern Alaska. I'm also an active member of the Tlingit Tribe."

"No offense, but I've never heard of you guys."

"None taken. We're mostly concentrated here in the Pacific Northwest. We don't sleep in teepees or eat cow hearts or anything like that."

They both laughed and continued their conversation for the rest of their drive. Mark had been apprehensive about Ethan, but genuinely enjoyed his company. They even almost forgot why they out there in the first place. The town wide search was supposed to last until ten, at which point the town had to be business as usual.

As Mark dropped Ethan off to his car at McHenry's, he caught another glimpse of Jimmy. This time the tears were gone and he was a man on a mission. He had his hunting buddies, all armed with their best rifles, and they prepared to continue their search with the police. Mark would have gone over to offer his condolences, but it felt too awkward at the moment. He'd catch up with Jimmy later.

The first few hours at work were strange. There was an intense solemnness in the air. Everyone made uneasy small talk, too afraid to utter what they were all thinking. By lunchtime this had subsided. Most of the guys were back to joking and laughing by that point. Mark, however, found no solace in humor or camaraderie. He couldn't get that scream out of his head.

Just then, another thought hit him hard like a train. The rifle he had dropped out in the woods by his cabin. Was it still there? Would someone find it and somehow link it to Kelly's disappearance? The entire rest of the day, Mark sweated with the thought of someone else finding that rifle. He wanted more than anything to say he was sick or find some reason to go home early and look for it. But they were already short with Barry in the hospital and a few hours behind. He'd be lucky if Tim didn't ask him to work late.

The entire rest of the day, Mark zoned out and just focused on his work with the precision of an automaton. He found that it made the day go by faster and helped him to keep calm. When the day finally ended, he clocked out quickly and avoided eye contact so as not to get caught up in a conversation.

Mark raced home and immediately grabbed his spare flashlight and headed out for the woods. It wasn't quite dusk yet, but he didn't know how long he would be out here. As he carefully attempted to retrace his steps, his thoughts juggled between finding the rifle and what would happen if that beast came back before he did. He tried putting the latter thought out of his mind.

To his surprise, Mark was better at tracking his own footprints than he thought. He followed them and in only twenty minutes he found the flashlight he dropped the night before. He clicked it on and it still worked fine. He slipped the spare one into his coat pocket and used this one, it was his favorite.

As Mark continued following his own footprints, he soon spotted the rifle on the ground. *Thank God, it's still here.* He ran over, picked it up, and slung it over his shoulder, holding onto it tightly this time. He looked around the area and realized it looked much less threatening in the daylight, even during a sunset. He then found something that disturbed him. Or rather what he *didn't* find was what disturbed him.

Mark looked around the entire area, including the spot where he had seen the piercing, red eyes the night before. There were no footprints but his anywhere in sight. Whatever animal was here had covered their prints or nothing was actually here. *I am losing my mind!* He couldn't figure out what was worse, a vicious animal that mauled Barry, kidnapped Kelly and doesn't leave tracks or the thought that this was all a hallucination of his.

"Kelly?!" a voice called out from the distance. Mark instantly jumped, startled. The voice called again, "Kelly, honey?!" It was Jimmy's. Mark followed the voice and spotted Jimmy, by himself, trekking through the woods with his rifle out. He spotted Mark and for a brief second a smile crept across his face. Immediately afterwards, he resumed his desperate look of despair.

"Jimmy, what are you doing all the way out here?" asked Mark, legitimately curious.

"I see that rifle I leant you came in handy, huh?" replied Jimmy, dodging the question.

"Yeah, went right for it when I knew I was coming out here. Where's the rest of the guys?"

"Ah, they all had to get home or work. It's been just me for the last few hours."

"Where are the police?"

"They say they're handling it, but they're just taking statements. I thought maybe if I just kept looking I'd get lucky. Maybe I'm just one look away from finding her."

Mark nodded, not knowing quite what to say to that. The pity he had for this poor man just trying to find his child left Mark depressed. He still couldn't say anything about the scream, but he could help Jimmy look in the very area he knew he heard it in. They spent another hour examining every broken twig, crushed leaf and scratched tree. Jimmy noticed all the footprints and asked, "This all you Mark?" Mark simply nodded and replied, "Yeah, been out here a while."

Finally when night fell, Mark convinced Jimmy to come inside to eat. He didn't have much to offer, but he felt that he owed this man, so he made his very best slightly burnt grilled cheese. They sat and ate in silence for a while, both exhausted in more ways than one. Finally, Jimmy just started talking.

"You go ahead and hang on to that rifle. Never know

when you may need it."

"Thanks Jimmy," replied Mark, figuring he kept bringing up the rifle to stop thinking about his daughter, even if just for a second.

"Listen, I know you walked all the way here, but I can give you ride back if you want."

"Thank you Mark, I think I'll do that."

"How are Caitlin and Sean?" asked Mark, knowing it might not be the best idea to ask about his other children, but he also wanted to make sure they were taken care of at the moment.

"They're getting by. Sean's back home, I didn't even send him to school today. Caitlin's running things at the bar, God bless her. I wasn't even gonna open today, but she didn't wanna lose a day of business and said 'Daddy, if we're open we can help the search party recharge when they come back.'"

"She's a good kid."

"After Molly died, I thought I was gonna be lost with three kids. But Caitlin's what holds our family together. She keeps Sean good in school and checks his homework and Kelly…"

Jimmy stopped there, as if he had almost forgotten what happened and then had a grim reminder. Mark could see the tears forming in his eyes. Jimmy quickly grabbed a napkin and wiped it off; embarrassed it would make him look weak. Mark put a reassuring hand on Jimmy's shoulder.

"I swear, if some psycho son of a bitch took my little girl…I'll cut his nuts off and put a bullet in his head."

"I hope it doesn't come to that, but if it does, I'll be right there with you."

They finished up dinner and Mark drove him back

39

to his house. Jimmy thanked Mark and walked over to the front door with Sean already waiting there since he saw the car. Mark had only ever met Sean once or twice, but he seemed to keep getting taller. *I don't remember growing that fast when I was ten.* Mark waved to Jimmy and drove back home.

For some reason, Mark's guilt seemed to dissipate. Maybe it was spending time and helping Jimmy or simply looking in the place he heard Kelly scream (assuming of course it *was* Kelly). He climbed into bed, and even though his mind was racing a million different thoughts, the pure exhaustion was enough to put him to sleep.

SIX

Mark glanced at the large, oak grandfather clock that decorated the corner of his office. It was an antique and he loved having it, but he always had the damnedest time making out the tiny Roman numerals and hands to determine the time. Across from him was Joe Thomas, the New York Governor, to whom he owed his entire career. Joe noticed him looking at the clock.

"I know, I *have* been here too long," laughed Joe.

"I'm sorry, I'm just tired."

"Ah, don't be. I don't think I've gotten a full night's sleep since I took this office. Not that I have any regrets. But, we can wrap up shortly. It's not every day we actually have a surplus on our hands."

"It is more fun than dealing with debt, I'll tell you that."

"I know I asked you last week to start thinking of where we could spend it, assuming spending it is the best option. If you thought it best, I wouldn't be opposed to saving it for a rainy day."

"I'd love to be able to save it, but word gets out we're holding money, it could look bad."

"Yeah, I guess you're right," Joe replied, hating the fact that he agreed.

"Could always put it in the retirement fund. If there's ever a shortage there you know they'll raise hell."

"And that's why the people of this great state elected you," complimented Joe, mostly glad that this meeting was over.

"Thanks Joe. Unless you have anything else…"

"No, I think that's it. I'm done bothering you. Oh, how's Livia? Heard she's writing a book."

"She's great, thanks. Yeah, she and a few law professors from Columbia are revising their Criminal Law textbook."

"Wow, sign me up for that when this miserable job ends," responded Joe, only half sarcastically.

They shook hands and Joe went back to his office on the other side of the building. Now that Mark was alone in his office, he was free to hyperventilate and sweat all he wanted at the stress the meeting had just put him through. If his office was equipped with a barf bag, he probably would have used it. A week earlier Joe had asked him to find a place for the surplus and he assumed it meant to spend or save it as he saw fit. After all, he was the comptroller and this specifically fell under his jurisdiction.

What Mark had failed to mention in the meeting with Joe, was that he had already transferred the five million surplus into the retirement fund and had successfully diverted $300,000 of it towards his own private account titled, "New York State Civil Service Seniority Fund". No one had noticed, and he was a third of his way to paying off his debt. He had run the numbers over and over again, and the accounts would correct themselves with interest in time.

He wasn't proud about doing what he simply called, "moving money around", but it was a means to an end. In an attempt to justify it, Mark frequently told himself that once his own debt problems were under control, he'd be a more efficient comptroller. Even he had trouble believing that one. Right or wrong, his plan would work. It had to. According to his calculations, he could pay off his debts in just five months and the state's money would be fully restored in eight, and no one would know the difference.

Many Americans find themselves waking up early on weekends simply out of habit and the fine tuning of their internal clock. Mark had read this somewhere and knew it to be completely true. It was Saturday and here he was, up before the crack of dawn. With everything going on in town and in his own mind, he didn't even bother trying to go back to sleep. He got up, got dressed and ate a quick breakfast.

Mark figured there would be another gathering at McHenry's to continue searching for Kelly. He checked his phone to see if anyone had called or texted with updates. There were none. He didn't know what to feel. She hadn't been found, but then again, neither had her corpse. As he walked out, he checked the scratches in the wall and thought they had grown even larger. *That's weird, didn't hear anything last night.* He had bigger concerns right now.

Just as he predicted, a crowd of volunteers had gathered at McHenry's. Though Mark had to admit it was smaller than he would have thought. There was Jimmy, Ethan, Caitlin and a few people Mark didn't know. They were each wearing their orange hunting vests and were equipped with flashlights and hiking supplies. Jimmy embraced Mark as he got out of his car.

"Thanks for coming out again."

"Just trying to do what I can."

With that, they were off into the vast expanse of the Alaskan wilderness. This region was technically categorized as a temperate rainforest. Mark had heard that when he moved here, but didn't really know or care what it meant. That was until he found himself scouring every square foot in the hopes of quelling the fears of a grief-stricken father. He wondered why there were no police out searching today and then realized he wasn't in New York anymore. This small town's only shot of finding her was citizens volunteering.

"That last night I saw her…weirdest thing happened," explained Jimmy, breaking the silence. Everyone's ears perked up and he continued, "Kelly wandered out into the woods and right before she did, she kept saying that she heard her mother calling her name."

As Jimmy spoke Mark could tell he was breaking down. Caitlin put her arm around her father and fought back tears herself. No one responded, mostly because none of them knew what to say to that. Occasionally, someone would attempt to make small talk, but the uncomfortable overtones remained. Eventually, they decided to split up and meet back at McHenry's by noon.

Mark and Ethan continued on through their section of the forest. They felt guilty and would never admit it, but both felt glad to be away from Jimmy for a bit. Watching him was almost unbearable. When he wasn't rambling on, he was silent with a worn and weathered look upon his face. But something he said stuck with Mark. The fact that Kelly claimed to hear her deceased mother calling her seemed frighteningly similar to Mark's incident that very same night.

"What'd you think about what Jimmy said?" inquired Mark, hoping to segue into his own experience.

"Which part?"

"About Kelly hearing her Mom call her. Was she imagining it? Was it some kidnapper?"

Ethan suddenly became very quiet and reserved. Considering his usual upbeat demeanor, this was quite strange. It was as if Mark had struck a nerve and didn't know how or why. Ethan opened up his mouth like he was going to speak, but then backed out at the last second and said nothing. It was clear that he was struggling to say what he was thinking about. Finally, he mustered up his courage and asked:

"Are you a superstitious person, Mark?"

"Well I *was* raised Catholic," chuckled Mark, not quite sure where this was going.

"I'm being serious," responded Ethan uncharacteristically stern. Mark was taken aback. "Well, I wouldn't say I'm superstitious, but I do think there are things out there that we can't explain."

"What if I told you that I don't think we'll find that poor little girl?"

"Why do you say that?" asked Mark, concerned at how this conversation was going.

"Have you ever heard of the Kushtaka?"

"The what?"

"It's called the Kushtaka, the most malevolent spirit in the Tlingit culture."

"Koosh...?"

"Don't. I'd rather not say its name any more than we have to," warned Ethan, legitimately afraid. He continued, "Growing up, my mother would tell me stories about this creature that looked like an otter but could change its shape. She always used to say that it would get me if I was bad. Belief in it is pretty split today and even those who don't believe in it would use it as a cautionary tale like my parents."

"So it's like the boogeyman?"

"That's oversimplifying it a bit, but yes. In all the old stories my mother told me, she always said that this creature would take the form of someone you knew, like your parents. Then it would call you into the forest and that's when it would get you."

"What happened then...in the stories?" asked Mark, starting to get frightened.

"Well let's just say there's a reason this spirit was worse than any other. Once it has you, it takes your very soul. You become a slave to it in the afterlife and can never find peace."

It took Mark a few moments to digest everything that Ethan had just told him. He had heard plenty of ghost stories from different cultures and religions, but this one really hit home. There was just too much going on this past week for it all to be mere coincidence. Mark was still hoping this was the case, but as each day and moment passed pessimism gained sway.

"Are you saying...?"

"I'm not sure what I'm saying Mark. I'm not even sure exactly what I believe in. I've never seen or witnessed anything like this before. But the way Jimmy told that story about Kelly hearing her mother just sounded too eerie and similar to the stories I was told growing up. For the sake of the girl, I hope none of them were true."

Mark considered opening up to Ethan and telling him everything. It seemed only fair as he had just risked ridicule by telling him about this Kushtaka creature. Ethan probably would have been more understanding than anyone else, considering what he had just revealed. Instead, Mark decided to still keep it to himself. After all the turmoil in his life, he didn't want to invite any more.

After they headed back for McHenry's at noon, Mark didn't talk much to anyone. He left for home as fast as he could, determined to find out everything he could. The more he thought about it, the more he realized this couldn't all be happenstance. The more he thought about his past, the more it made sense. The truth was he *did* remember strange occurrences in his house as a child. After his father's suicide and mother's suicide attempt, he blocked out a great deal. But the more he looked back and tried to remember, he couldn't help but feel like someone or something had been watching him. That feeling had especially come back within the last week.

As soon as he got through his front door, he had his computer open and Googled "Kushtaka". For the next few hours, he explored the myriad of links that Google presented him; everything from a semi-useful Wikipedia article to blogs and 'sightings'. The deeper he dug into the research and folklore, the more alarmed he became.

Much of what he read corroborated everything that Ethan had told him. The stories of the Kushtaka claimed they were in the business of stealing souls and draining their victims from an everlasting life.

According to the myths and legends, death was a suitable alternative. As for their methods and abilities, Mark found that they were known for their shape-shifting. While they were commonly associated with otters ("Kushtaka" itself translated to "land-otter man") they could take the form of a much larger animal, if necessary.

Surprisingly, he even found a few myths about the Kushtaka helping sailors and fisherman lost at sea. But just as he was entertaining the thought of this creature being benevolent, he read deeper and made a horrific discovery. In all these stories it would certainly save said victim from drowning and then enslave their soul from there. The Tlingit and Tsimshian peoples of the Pacific Northwest considered the Kushtaka to be the most frightening and dangerous spirits. Mark could hardly disagree with them.

This opened up the mental floodgates to a sea of new questions. Could this have been what scratched up the wall? Could this have been what mauled Barry? Was this the voice Mark heard in the darkness calling his name? Was this what made Kelly disappear? And most importantly, was it after him?

That last thought didn't sit particularly well with Mark. Any other time, he never would have even considered this an option; and probably would have shot down anyone who suggested that it was. Just then that awful old feeling of being watched came back. He got up and closed all the curtains around the cabin, effectively blocking the sunlight. Despite doing this, he still couldn't shake this feeling.

Just when he had successfully psyched himself out, Mark's cell phone rang and caused him to jump nearly a foot in the air. As he caught his breath and looked down at the number, he was given another startle. It was Livia's old number. *What the hell is she calling me for?* He slowly reached for the phone, debating whether or not to answer. If he did, it would be awkward. If he didn't, she'd probably leave a voicemail, then he'd have to call her back and that would be worse. Mark took a deep breath and answered his phone.

"Hello?"

"Hi Mark," greeted Livia, in a tone devoid of any emotion.

A few seconds passed of silence.

"How've you been?" asked Mark, hoping she would reveal the purpose of her call.

"It's your mother. Now she's all right. But she's gotten worse."

"How bad?"

"She was almost arrested for disorderly conduct because she was shouting profanity at teenagers in the park."

One unforeseen consequence of Mark's debacle that led to him moving across the country was the welfare of his mother. When he took off, she had recently been diagnosed with dementia. He told himself, and her, that he would occasionally come back to Buffalo to check in on her. He was not proud to admit that he hadn't visited nor given so much as a phone call. Naturally, he assumed Livia knew all this already and would, at some point dish out a thinly veiled insult regarding it.

"Where is she now?" inquired Mark, honestly concerned and feeling quite guilty.

"She's at home. But Mark, I think she's at the point where she can't live by herself anymore."

"I understand."

A few more seconds of silence passed. Both of them knew exactly what they wanted to say to the other, but struggled to bring themselves to do it. Finally it was Livia that went first:

"Listen Mark, I'm only involved in this because I care about your mother. Please don't think..."

"I don't. Trust me, I understand. But thank you for calling me. I know it probably wasn't easy."

"Well I'm still listed as an emergency contact. How soon can you get out here?"

"Soon as I can. I'll shoot for tomorrow, if not Monday."

"I'll keep an eye on her for now, but when you get here, I won't be..."

"I know. Listen, how have you been? How's Joe doing?"

"I really don't think you get to ask that. I have to run, goodbye."

She ended the call just as snappily as she delivered that last line to Mark. For a few moments, his ex-wife had made him completely forget about the potential Kushtaka haunting and reminded him of the incredible guilt he had from his divorce, leaving his mother and resigning his job. He wasn't sure which one was worse. The entire time he had been in Alaska, it had been so easy for him to just forget about his past.

Immediately, he minimized all the tabs regarding the Kushtaka and tried to find the cheapest and soonest flight. There was one leaving that night, but far out of his price range. He found another for less than $400, but that didn't leave for another month and would require at least one layover. Mark continued to search every deal website he could remember from those incredibly cheesy commercials with actors past their prime. Finally, he found a cheap flight that left at Monday morning at six. He booked it immediately. Oddly enough, he spotted this flight as a pop-up ad; as if some unseen force brought it to his attention.

The rest of the night was spent packing and getting ready for his trip. Mark meant to call his mother and check in on her, but could never bring himself to do it. He wasn't sure why. Maybe it was fear that Livia would answer and he would have to speak with her again. Maybe he felt better worrying about her because it took his mind off his current demonic predicament. Whichever the case, fear won out over guilt and he settled that he would talk to his mother the next day.

Mark downed a few tablespoons of NyQuil before eight-thirty, hoping it would help him fall asleep sooner. Something told him that trying to sleep alone in this cabin would prove difficult tonight, knowing what he did. His mind kept going back to everything he read about the Kushtaka. Then again, assuming this thing was even real, why hadn't it attacked him? There were plenty of opportunities. Hell, he even ran out into the woods and dropped his rifle and flashlight. If anyone or anything wanted to decimate his body and steal his soul, that would have been the opportune moment.

As he lay in bed, he waited anxiously for the sound of claws or heavy footprints outside his cabin. He even kept the rifle loaded and on the floor next to the bed, just in case. Mark still wasn't sure he even believed in this thing, but being prepared never hurt. The night was eerily quiet. As time went on, he slowly let his guard down and drifted off to sleep.

SEVEN

Little Mark sat up in bed, unable to fall asleep. Mommy had tucked him in forever ago and told him not to come out of his room. He had been doing that way too often and it made Daddy nervous. He thought about that day last week when he went down into Daddy's office and saw those weird candles and that book that Daddy was reading. He thought it was just a dream, but now he thought maybe it was real. His face had been sore the next day from when Daddy slapped him.

He shivered as he pulled the comforter over his shoulders. All of a sudden, it got really cold in his room. Why did this keep happening every night? Then little Mark looked over on his bedpost, afraid of what he knew he'd see. The rosary that Mommy had given him, which hung on the post, started to rise up in the air like someone picked it up, but there was no one there. Suddenly, the rosary flew across the room and hit the wall with a loud crack. It made little Mark jump every time.

That was the third time that happened this week. Then came the three knocks on the wall, like they always did. Little Mark was terrified, now shivering because he was so scared. Sometimes Mommy would come in and tell him to stop making a racket and he'd feel better not being alone. He wanted to tell someone, but the last time he told Daddy, he yelled at him and said he was just imagining things. Little Mark crawled under his comforter and prayed, "Our Father who art in Heaven, hallowed be thy name..." hoping that either God or this blanket would protect him from whatever was out there.

"I know what you did Mark!" shouted a voice from the distance, startling Mark awake. It was early, still very dark. Just as he was trying to get his bearings, the voiced called out again, "How could you do this to me Mark!" There was no mistaking it that time. The voice belonged to Joe Thomas, still the current governor of New York and a man that Mark hoped to never run into again. Mark called out into the darkness, "Shut up!"

Now it was daylight and Mark woke up for a second time. Had that been a dream? Had it been the NyQuil? He didn't spend too much time worrying about this as he got up and got dressed. He had lived in this cabin for six months now and had never set foot in the town's church, but there was a first time for everything. He knew there would be a vigil for Kelly and he wanted to be there to support Jimmy. This was especially so, knowing that he'd have to go back to Buffalo for a few days and the rest of the town would be there.

As he drove towards the church, he saw that the parking lot was filled beyond capacity, and that many had simply parked on the street or even in the shopping center nearby. *I guess more than the usual crowd showed up today.* After parking and crossing the street, Mark looked down at his khaki pants and polo shirt. Now he was concerned that he could be underdressed for church. He didn't even remember the last time he had gone, let alone what was appropriate to wear.

Creaking open the old, wooden, worn out doors, Mark figured this place hadn't been renovated, or even inspected in a long time. When he entered the church, he realized the situation was just as bad inside as out. There were absolutely no seats left and many were standing and leaning up against the walls. Mark picked out what looked like a comfortable place and rested his shoulders on it.

Next to the altar sat a large easel and on it a picture of Kelly with her family and one by herself. *Is this her funeral?* Mark hated even thinking it, but he knew that this very well could be the closure that Jimmy needed to go on if they never found her. Of course there would be an actual funeral once she was legally declared dead, but this is the one that would be remembered most. And just as he contemplated the significance of the event, he noticed most other men around him dressed in shirts and ties. *Shit, knew I should have unpacked my good suit.*

Mark then remembered the last time he went to church. During his comptroller election campaign, he regularly attended mass simply to make connections and gain votes. He had never really just sat (or in this case stood) and listened to the service or took in his surroundings. They had all been more akin to business deals. He couldn't even see where Jimmy was sitting at the moment, but it didn't matter. He was here for him nevertheless.

The priest came out and began the mass. He was

tall and lean, with slicked back hair and a handsome face. Mark was taken aback at just how young he looked. *He looks more like a frat boy than a priest.*
They went through all the usual rituals of a Catholic Mass. Mark was surprised at how much he remembered. Next came a carefully chosen Bible reading from Matthew 19:14 ("Let the little children come to me").

After that came a sermon that was much more specific to Kelly, Jimmy and their entire family. The priest thanked all the volunteers helping with the search and urged everyone to not give up hope, and to also pray that her soul may find heaven should it come to that. It was a strange service that seemed like both a memorial and a rallying call to optimism.

When the service was over, most of the crowd approached Jimmy to give their support. As the pews were thinned out, Mark spotted Tim. He knew that this was probably not the most appropriate time to talk to him about this, but he was leaving in the morning and needed to clear it. As Mark walked up to Tim, he was concerned by the intense look on Tim's face. It was as if he had news of his own.

"Hey Tim."

"Mark."

"How's uh, how's Barry doing?"

"Actually, I wanted to talk to you about it." Tim sighed and put his hand on his forehead.

Don't even tell me that bastard died on us.

Tim continued, "I just talked to the hospital before coming here. He's in a coma. Something about he developed an infection from the gash on his chest. They don't know when …if he wakes up."

"Shit, I'm sorry to hear," exclaimed Mark, widening his eyes when he realized he had just cursed in a church.

"Look Mark, I'm really gonna need your help this week. I still have to leave. I only extended my notice a week with Barry's accident, but I'm still moving. This week I'm gonna be interviewing somebody to replace me."

"What about for Barry's job?"

"Well that's where I was hoping you'd come in. How do you feel about doing Barry's job?"

"Temporarily or...?"

"Even if Barry makes it, I don't see him coming back to work for years at least. You don't have to answer now. Is a week fair?"

Mark nodded. A week to decide was perfectly fair. Mark was still in disbelief over Barry's condition. Now it seemed almost likely that he would die, or least spend the rest of his life in a hospital bed. Something hit very hard about all this. This Kushtaka creature seemed much too real and potent now that it could permanently ruin or end lives. And there was still the matter of poor little Kelly. Would she ever be found?

"Listen Tim," began Mark, dreading what he had to say next, mostly for the timing.

"Yeah?"

"I'm definitely willing to think about the job. And I'm sorry for springing this on you now but...I need off till Wednesday or Thursday."

Tim's expression went so quickly from surprise to frustration to understanding that it could have set a record.

"It's my mom," explained Mark, trying to justify it,

"Odds are I've gotta check her into a nursing home. So I have fly out for a few days and take care of things. When I get back I'll do everything I can to help you."

"Do what you have to and get back as soon as you can."

They shook hands. Mark was glad that Tim's reaction was now one less issue he'd have to deal with. Then again, there wasn't much Tim could really do. He'd been living here half a year, completely eventless, and now all hell decided to break loose in the same week. He walked over to Jimmy and gave him a few supporting words. After that, he started to head out and noticed the priest walking outside.

For some strange reason, an idea hit Mark like a slap in the head. He needed to talk to the priest. Although he seemed young, and probably inexperienced, this clergyman could be the solution to one of his problems. He rushed outside and spotted him standing next to the sign changing the letters and numbers to update the mass times. Mark walked over and simply struck up a conversation.

"They got you doing that yourself?"

The priest chuckled and replied, "See what happens when you take a job for the money?"

Mark extended his hand and introduced himself. The priest smiled and did the same.

"Father Hauser, but my friends call me Eric."

"Don't take this the wrong way, but are you fresh out of school or something?"

Hauser chuckled, "That obvious, huh? Just graduated seminary two years ago."

"From around here?" asked Mark, starting to notice

Hauser's accent.

"Nah, Long Island actually."

"Really?"

"I know what you're thinking, right? Let's just say you don't usually pick where they send you, and they like to play favorites."

Father Hauser didn't seem like any priest Mark had ever met. Hell, he was tempted to call him Son Hauser given his age. Mark went on to explain his situation, leaving out a few major details. He told Hauser that he had recently moved there, and just hadn't gotten around to attending church and wanted him to bless his house. He could tell Hauser knew he was partially full of shit, but didn't fret over it. He agreed to come over later than afternoon to do the blessing.

Mark went home feeling somewhat accomplished. He had cleared his days off with work and would soon have some headway into his "other" problem. It sounded cliché, but simply having a priest bless the place would make him feel more at ease. His mind drifted to Barry for a while, wondering if he'd pull through. Even just being stuck in a coma seemed like hell to Mark. His greatest fear was always being trapped and not being able to do a damn thing about it. *Kind of like now, huh?*

He checked the time and realized that it was now evening over in Buffalo. There was a phone call he'd been dreading, but knew that now was the ideal time to make it. She'd be awake, preparing for dinner if not already eating and in a rush to get him off the phone. That was his hope of course. Mark picked up his phone, dialed in the number and his finger hovered over the call button for a few seconds. Taking a deep breath, he pressed it, knowing there was no turning back.

"Hello?" inquired an old, tired and quite familiar voice.

"Mom, it's Mark. How are you?"

"Mark? Aren't you supposed to be at work?"

"No Mom, it's Sunday."

"Sunday? Well did you go to church? I didn't see you."

"Yeah, actually I did go today. Must have missed you, I was sitting way in the back."

"Oh, well what'd you do that for? You know I like the front row."

Her condition had worsened in the months he was gone. Mark could honestly only recall calling her twice since his move. It left him with incredible guilt, but as he listened to her ramble and try to get a grasp on reality, it was almost too much to bear. For most of his life, she was all he had. He couldn't remember that much about his father. The last week though, he'd had the most vivid dreams bringing back those old memories. It prompted him to change the subject to something his mother may have known a little more about.

"Hey Mom?"

"Yes Mark?"

"What does Dad keep in his office?"

"Well son, you know how upset your father gets when you go in there."

"I know, but do you know what he keeps in there? There was this weird book."

"You stay out of your father's room and that's final!"

This sudden anger took him by surprise. He

remembered that before his father went to the hospital his parents fought a lot, more than usual. He never knew about what, and couldn't remember most of what went on back then. Maybe he had witnessed something traumatic, or maybe he was just too young for his brain to form long lasting memories. Either way, it was one mystery he intended to solve while out there. He couldn't quite explain it, but he now felt drawn to the idea of knowing.

They spoke for about another twenty minutes. He found out that her neighbor was cooking dinner for her, and he told her to thank this person on his behalf. He was certain that she wouldn't be able to live on her own anymore. But he was only giving himself three days to do what would most likely take weeks. There wasn't just the task of moving her, there was emptying her apartment and making sure she was settled He hadn't told Tim this, but he figured he'd have to fly out more often and maybe even stay for weeks at a time.

He let her go when she said that dinner was ready, and was glad he made the call. He knew there was no making up for everything he had done in his past, but this was a start. Getting out there could clear his head of everything happening here, and could lead to patching things up with Livia. It was obvious that they would never be married or really close to each other again, but he would settle for polite acquaintances.

Around six, Father Hauser pulled up in his used Hyundai and got out, dressed in the typical black shirt, white collar garb. He carried a Bible and an aspergillum filled with holy water. Mark opened the door and greeted him,

"Thanks for coming out."

"Oh no, thank *you*. This is actually my first house blessing."

"How about that?"

Mark wasn't sure how he felt about having a priest so inexperienced; especially one who was so nonchalant about admitting it. Hauser took out his "cheat sheet" which contained the step by step process of how to do a house blessing. It was almost funny how much he reeked of amateur and didn't even bother trying to hide it. He walked room to room, sprinkling holy water and reciting the prayer. Mark watched intently, half expecting something strange to happen.

Hauser finished his blessing and smiled. "And that's how it's done. Thanks Mark. I feel like the real deal now," he said never letting up on his frat boy persona. Mark was just glad to have had something done. If this Kushtaka was real, maybe this would keep it at bay. Just then, Hauser threw his head back as a torrent of blood rushed out of his nose. Mark ran and grabbed a roll of paper towels and handed it to him.

"What the hell, you all right?" he asked, more curious than concerned to be honest.

Hauser had managed to stop the flow and was now patting and wiping up blood off his face. Mark could tell he was embarrassed to hand him these used paper towels that looked like a crime scene.

"I don't know. That's never happened to me before."

They cleaned up and Hauser went to the bathroom to wash off his face. Mark was perplexed. This could have all just been a coincidence, but some strange one it would be. Then again, nothing he read about Kushtaka said anything about violent nosebleeds. That almost seemed like something more out of Poltergeist. Mark chalked it up to the high altitude, since he was used to Long Island. That was his explanation and he was sticking with it.

Hauser left, not saying much after coming out of the bathroom. Mark didn't really mind, but he could tell the young guy was humiliated. His cool guy persona had been blown by a combination of low pressure and possibly something supernatural. Mark hoped it was only the pressure, and focused the rest of the night on packing.

By eight, he had two suitcases ready to go. One was filled with clothes, the other with other effects he might need. He wasn't sure why, but he left one intentionally half empty. Something told him that he may be bringing a few things back with him. It was as if he was developing a sixth sense. He had enough on his mind to freak him out, so he tried not to dwell on this one too much.

Right before getting to bed early, he called Paul and asked for a ride to the airport in the morning. It was a long ride so when Paul agreed, Mark promised him breakfast as compensation. He slid into the covers and checked the side of the bed to ensure the rifle was right where he left it, just in case the blessing wasn't enough to protect the place. Right before Mark fell asleep, he could swear he heard a wolf howling. It sounded much too close for comfort.

EIGHT

Mark lay back in bed, eyes glued to the massive LED TV mounted on his wall. The salesman who sold it to him said that the picture would be so clear it would feel like he was actually there. *They don't mention that you can also see every wrinkle and blemish on people's faces.* This was a rare opportunity for him. Most days he was lucky to be home by eight-thirty and by then he was exhausted. But he had gotten a lot done today and felt he deserved a break. So he came home a few hours early and was catching up on this mindless reality TV that seemed to grip the masses. It was stupid as hell, but he had to admit it was entertaining.

"Hey Mark?" called Livia from the other room, paying bills.

"Yeah?" responded Mark, partly zoning her out.

"What's this statement from?"

"Which statement?" inquired Mark as he jumped up, immediately alert.

Mark looked at himself in the mirror to ensure he was composed and then walked into the kitchen with Livia. She was sitting at a table strewn with bills, envelopes, receipts and other papers. *Is she paying bills or doing our damn taxes?* She handed him the statement in question and he instantly recognized it. The account was titled "New York State Civil Service

Seniority Fund". So far it had reached $3.2 million dollars, a considerable increase from the $900,000 Mark initially needed to get out of debt.

"That one from work?" asked Livia, seemingly benign.

"Yeah, I don't know how that got in with our personal stuff. I'm sorry," answered Mark as he took the statement before Livia could read any more of it.

"Kinda small for a retirement fund isn't it?"

"It's for one of the supervisors. They don't like us putting their names on it."

"Okay."

It was obvious that Livia found this situation peculiar. But as long as it was for the wrong reasons, Mark was fine. She had never known about the debt, or the fact that he had already paid it off months ago. He had originally intended to stop then, but he still felt the need to have something for a rainy day. Day by day, week by week, it became easier to divert money into this phony account. But now he had over three times as much as he originally needed. He couldn't spend too much or they'd notice. He couldn't return it all or they'd notice. Mark Pallano was truly lost.

There was no need for his alarm as Mark woke up at four on his own. He hadn't slept all night. He hadn't had this much on his mind since…the last time he saw Livia in person. By four-thirty, Paul was knocking on the door, and Mark let him in. They ate a very early breakfast with a cup of coffee and were on their way.

As Mark stepped outside, he was unnerved by the eerie darkness that accompanied the night just before dawn. It was also darkest then, and a dense fog drifted through the air.   Mark wondered what abominable creature or creatures could lurk in this darkness, waiting to pounce as it likely had on Barry. Much to Mark's relief, they quickly stepped into Paul's jeep and drove off.

"It's gonna be rough this week without you man, not gonna lie," commented Paul, trying to make small talk and not realizing how this might come off.

"I know. It's just bad timing."

"I'm sorry. I didn't mean it like that."

Mark shook his head to show he took no offense. He appreciated the ride, but really wasn't in the mood for small talk. Paul must have taken the hint from either Mark's tone or body language because he didn't talk much the rest of the ride. He might have also have just been too tired. Either way, it worked for Mark. He wasn't sure what he dreaded more, seeing his mother or seeing Livia.

They pulled up to the departure gate and Mark got out so he could get his bag from the backseat. Paul then got out seeing if he needed a hand. As Mark swung his large and heavy bag, his boarding pass fell out of his coat pocket and landed on the ground. Paul reached down and picked it up for him, unintentionally catching a glance of what was written on it. Mark froze, hoping Paul didn't read any of it, despite it being right in front of his face.

"You're going to Buffalo? Thought you said you were going home to Philly."

"Layover. The direct flight was way more."

Paul nodded nonchalantly and handed Mark his pass. He wasn't trying to be inquisitive or nosy. Most likely, he picked it up to be nice and just happened to see it. The rest was mere curiosity. Mark was just glad that his destination was easier to explain than why his last name was listed as "Pallano" versus "Taylor". Only Barry knew that from seeing his documents for employment.

Mark thanked Paul, they shook hands, and he was off. He drifted through security and boarding, not really taking in his surroundings; partly because of his lack of sleep and partly because of everything on his mind. Once the plane was in the air, he noticed a strange sensation. The ominous foreboding that he had become accustomed to in Alaska began to dissipate. The farther the plane took him from Juneau, the clearer his head became. One small part of it remained, however. He couldn't shake the feeling that something was still watching him, albeit it was more dormant now.

Six hours later and Mark was just waking up again. He never thought he'd fall asleep with these bear traps they called seats, but sometimes exhaustion trumps everything. He gazed out the window as the plane touched ground. The air even smelled different now. Then again, that might have just been the plane's recirculation system he smelled. Either way, it reminded him of home.

He got off the plane, bags in hand and made for the car rental place attached to the airport. Losing all of his money did have one advantage; he didn't have to waste time making a selection. Whichever car was cheapest, had four wheels and worked would be his choice. Mark wound up with a used Ford from the early 2000's. Not bad, and he'd only be using it for three days.

It was already four in the afternoon in Buffalo and Mark needed to get started immediately. As he drove away from the airport, Mark made a mental list of everything he needed to accomplish with this trip. Today all he needed to do was check in with his mother and he'd be staying in her apartment anyway. Tomorrow was going to be the long day. He had to visit nursing homes, find one that fit his mother right and start cleaning out her apartment. He'd have Livia to help him, which she was doing only for his mother's sake.

Mark was astounded at how he still remembered his way around town, long after leaving. It really did all come back. Fortunately, he had found his mother an apartment in his old neighborhood of Williamsville. It wasn't cheap, but it was a decent area and he knew she'd be all right there living on her own...until now. It wasn't far from the airport and he was there within twenty minutes. She had been expecting him, but given her condition, he was prepared to expect anything.

As he got out of the car with his bags, he took notice of an all too familiar car in the parking lot. *I guess we're getting that awkward introduction out of the way early.* He sighed as he walked up to the front door, preparing an opening statement that was both assertive and neutral for his now ex-wife. The divorce had only been finalized a month or so earlier. Mustering up his courage, he rang the bell labeled "Pallano".

"Who is it?" asked his mother through the intercom.

"Mom, it's me Mark. I'm here."

"Mark? I thought you were working. Why aren't you

at work?"

"Cause I'm here to see you, but I can't get in."

"Here just hit this button," declared another voice from the intercom. When Mark heard it he cringed.

The loud buzzer rang and Mark was able to open the door. He walked down the hallway to his mother's door, which was already open. His elderly mother embraced him with a smile and a hug. This affection actually felt really good. He had forgotten how cold and distant he had become since he moved.

"Well, are you just gonna stand out here?" asked his mother, with a hint of sass.

"You're blocking the way," responded Mark playfully.

As he walked into her apartment and shut the door, he was hit by a cold gaze from Livia standing in the kitchen. She gave him a smile, but one that was so insincere she might not have even bothered. He returned said smile and the two greeted each other with mutual passive aggressive feelings of despising. Mark put down his bag and walked his mother over to the couch. Despite her mental state, she seemed to be doing well physically. As he attempted to hold her arm, she resisted and walked herself. She had always been a strong and independent woman...at least since Mark was ten.

Once he got her settled and turned on the TV, Mark walked over into the kitchen to have a word with Livia. While he dreaded this, he did need an update. She was in one of her usual designer pantsuits and here he was in jeans, a t-shirt and a worn out winter coat. That, along with his new beard and longer, uncombed hair, must have been quite a shock to Livia. Her double take after seeing him said more than words ever could.

"How's she doing?" he asked, attempting to be as neutral as possible.

"Today was a good day. But she has a habit of wandering off, leaving the door wide open or sometimes she'll leave the stove on and forget about it. Physically she's fine, but she really needs…"

"I know."

Livia was visibly upset by her former mother-in-law's situation. The two of them had always gotten along. Mark was an only child so his mother never had a daughter. He wondered how bizarre it must have been for the two of them to keep in touch during his absence. He was grateful that Livia still seemed to really care about his mother. It was comforting to know that he could get the process started and rely on her to follow up.

"Hey listen, thanks for helping out," Mark whispered soothingly, putting a hand on her shoulder.

"I don't do it for you," replied Livia coldly as she recoiled from his hand.

"Either way, I appreciate it."

"I have to get going. I'll be in the area until Friday, then I've got to fly back to New York City."

"Well, I'm here till Wednesday. So I'll try to have a place picked out by then. I may need you to…"

"I know. I'll handle it. Your mother shouldn't suffer just because…"

She stopped herself before saying something she'd regret. With that, she gathered up her things and was out the door, leaving Mark and his mother for a night of bonding. They worked together and made a delicious spaghetti dinner. For a bit, Mark forgot what he was there to do. It was just pleasant spending the evening with someone other than a drunken coworker with a sob story and surly attitude.

After dinner, they sat back and relaxed on the couch. Occasionally, his mother would get confused about things like the date and current events. But most of their discussion was about Mark's childhood. She reminisced about the time he scored the winning goal for his soccer team or when he was elected class president. The last fond memory was him becoming New York State comptroller. It was amazing how vivid this memory was. It must have been important to her.

"You having a good time working with the governor? Isn't he your friend?"

"Yeah Mom, it's great. He's my best friend," answered Mark, not having the heart to tell her truth. Technically, what he was saying *was* true, just not for the last six months.

For some strange reason, Mark kept thinking about his father. It had been years since he had talked about him or actively thought about him, but Mark was almost certain he had been dreaming about it. It had always been a touchy subject with his mother, especially when he was younger. The prevailing story he had been told was that his father was schizophrenic and killed himself to finally make the voices stop. *Between that and Mom's dementia, I don't have a chance, do I?*

"Hey Mom, do you remember that time we went up to Niagara Falls and rode the boat? It was me, you and Dad, remember?"

"I remember getting soaked," replied his mother, now

apprehensive of his question.

"Mom, whatever happened to Dad?"

"I told you Mark, his brain was sick and he died. It was very hard on you. On both of us."

"Do you remember how he'd always get mad when I went into his office?"

"You shouldn't be going in there Mark! How many times do I have to tell you?!" she shouted.

Mark was taken aback. Her response brought back old memories, one of which involved his father slapping him. He couldn't believe he had forgotten about it. He apologized for bringing it up and his mother returned to normal as if nothing had happened. She was pleasant after that and the two of them enjoyed each other's company for the rest of the evening. His mother went to bed early, around quarter to nine and he followed suit shortly after. He remembered one of the selling points of this place was the sofa bed. When he pulled off the cushions, he was glad to see it was still there.

After putting a set of sheets and a pillow on the sofa bed, Mark lay down and relaxed. He was physically exhausted, but not enough to fall asleep, apparently. His mind went back to that question about his father. Mark had yet to admit this, not even to himself, but he had an ulterior motive for coming back to Buffalo. It wasn't just to get away from work, though that was a bonus. He was determined to do everything he could during these three days to dig up the truth about his father. What was he involved in? Why was it so secretive and ultimately, why did he kill himself? Finally, after the exhaustion cleared his head, Mark fell asleep.

NINE

Little Mark knocked on the bathroom door for the third time. Why wasn't Mommy answering? She told him she was taking a bath and not to bother her. He didn't want to make her upset, but it was dinner time and he was getting really hungry. Little Mark was seven years old now. The last year had been pretty rough, especially for Mommy. She hadn't really been the same since Daddy died.

He knocked again calling, "Mommy? Are you okay in there?" He reached for the doorknob and it opened. That was weird since Mommy always locked it. As he walked in, he saw Mommy lying back in the bath tub. She was sound asleep. "Mommy?" called little Mark, hoping she was just taking a nap. When she didn't respond, little Mark got worried. He walked over and tapped her on the shoulder. "Mommy?" he called again, this time with tears swelling in his eyes.

This went on for a few minutes and little Mark started to panic. He almost tripped on all the medicine bottles on the floor next to the tub. What were they doing there? Little Mark may have only been seven, but he knew something wasn't right. He ran into the other room and picked up the phone. His teacher from school had told him that if there was ever an emergency, he should dial 911. As little Mark dialed the number, he started to sob and hoped whoever answered could understand him.

Still on Alaska Time, Mark awoke at almost noon. He sat up and saw his mother sitting on the chair next to the couch watching some game show rerun. She took notice of her son and simply nodded and said, "I think you're gonna be late for work." Mark slowly got up and groggily made his way into the kitchen. His breakfast options were a bowl of cereal, oatmeal or toast. Not all that different than what he was currently used to.

As Mark washed the toast down with a cup of coffee, he sighed at realizing all the things that needed to get done today. Livia had set up appointments with three nursing homes in the afternoon. Obviously, Mark wanted only the best for his mother, but given his current financial situation, it would have to be a place that accepted Medicare. His old job (even minus the embezzlement) probably would have paid for round the clock care right here in her apartment. The more he thought about it, the worse it made him feel. *How the hell did it come to this?*

After breakfast, Mark got dressed and noticed a message on his phone. Apparently, he would be going to the first place by himself. She wouldn't be able to meet up with him until at least three-thirty. It didn't matter; in fact maybe it was better this way. Mark couldn't quite describe how torn he was between wanting Livia's help versus never wanting to see or speak to her again. It wasn't even her fault, he had been in the wrong, and that guilt only made it worse.

He gave his mother a kiss on the forehead, as she stared mesmerized into the TV and left. Mark still knew his way around Buffalo and this first address concerned him a bit. He wasn't positive, but he vaguely remembered where this neighborhood was located. As he got closer and drove by police tape and chalk outline, he knew his suspicions were correct.

The facility was actually pretty nice and was simply the victim of its own location. Mark knew what to look for. He saw the nurses actively making rounds and checking in on residents. He walked by a common room and saw an excited volunteer playing bingo and thought his mother would love it here. What he did not like, however, was learning the price tag after sitting down with the administrator.

"We can of course, still accept social security checks as a portion of monthly payment. Quite a few of our residents' families do the same," explained the administrator, as he adjusted his hundred dollar tie and checked the time on his Rolex. Mark was in no mood to tell this guy why he couldn't possibly afford this place. He simply shook the man's hand, thanked him for his time and said he would consider it.

The second place looked much nicer on the outside, but once inside, Mark knew there was no way he was bringing his mother here, even if they paid him too. He walked by an old woman sitting in a wheelchair unattended in the hallway. In the common area, he spotted a man that had urinated himself and was just sitting in it. Mark nearly threw up at the smell when walking by several rooms, and the entire time had not spotted a single staff member. He left without checking in for his appointment and considered making an anonymous tip to the Health Department.

As he was driving back from the hellhole, he got a

call from Livia, who was now free to meet at the third place. *Can't be any worse than the last one.* This next facility was actually highly recommended. He remembered knowing someone whose uncle had been here and he was impressed. But that was over fifteen years ago. Mark certainly knew how much things could change in even in just a few months.

He and Livia met in the parking lot. She seemed friendlier than last night. It was clear that she was making an effort to be civil and Mark would try and do the same. After all, this was *his* mother she was helping. He appreciated that Livia still cared, even if not for him. It just pained him to be around her. Mark hated being reminded of everything that happened.

As the Director of Nursing gave them a tour, Livia took the lead in firing question after question about the standards of care, budgets, staff-to-resident ratio and a million other things. *Always the lawyer with her.* For a brief second, Mark remembered what had attracted him to Livia in the first place. Beside her undeniably stunning beauty, she was a force to be reckoned with. She could break down a hardened Mafioso on the witness stand.

This place wasn't bad. It had been the best one he had seen today, then again, that wasn't saying much. But the staff was friendly, the residents looked taken care of and best of all, it was within the price range. As Mark gazed around each hallway and room, half listening to Livia's interrogation, he couldn't help but feel a slight sadness. He knew that once he checked his mother into this place, most likely she would eventually die within these walls.

Afterwards, the two of them stopped for an early

dinner before heading over to the storage facility. It was a task neither was looking forward to. Much to Mark's surprise, Livia picked a burger place nearby. They had gone on a date there back when they were getting to know each other in law school. He wasn't sure if she remembered, but a small part of him hoped she did.

As Livia ordered up at the counter, Mark sat in a booth and called his mother to check in. She had gone from watching old game shows to doing her crossword puzzles. Mark had gotten her a giant book of them for Christmas. He had heard that it was good for dementia and wanted to do everything she could to at least slow it down. Mark wasn't sure if there was any science to that, but was more than willing to give it a shot.

Before she even walked over, Mark's nostrils were hit by the aroma of fresh burgers. This place had always been great. Livia sat down and actually smiled as she handed Mark his food. This one actually looked happy, not like the obligatory half smile, half frown she gave him the night before when he arrived. Mark never would have guessed this in the months prior, but he and Livia sat and enjoyed each other's company.

Mark asked her how everything was going, and she had done quite well since he left. She had finished that book and was being considered for a teaching position at Columbia Law School. The conversation then shifted to her going back and forth between Manhattan and Buffalo to check in on Mark's mother. She seemed frustrated when Mark asked how she planned to do this.

"Mark, why not just move back here?" she asked, matter-of-factly.

"I don't know if I can," replied Mark, not sure how to respond.

Mark hadn't honestly considered it because at this point he didn't really see it as an option. It was a nice break to get away from his problems in his new home, but he was still left with an ominous feeling that he didn't belong here. The last six months had been an exercise in loneliness, yet Alaska had made him feel safe from all of his old problems. This was of course, until the last week when he started developing new ones. Maybe Livia had a point.

"Well, they're actually promoting me to management," explained Mark, trying to think of a reason not to move. At this point he was just playing devil's advocate for himself.

"Seriously Mark? Where do you work out there?"

"It's a lumber mill."

"What the hell are you doing working with a bunch of drunks and losers? How far down the ladder did you have to go? You were comptroller for God's sakes."

"Not anymore."

"Think about what's best for you mother," suggested Livia, now in a sympathetic tone.

"I am. I just thought that...well I thought you wouldn't want me here."

"Mark," sighed Livia, shaking her head, "what happened happened. There's nothing you or I can do about that now. I may not be very happy with you right now and I may never be again. That's why I divorced you and you were lucky I didn't prosecute you. But where in the hell did you get the idea that you had to move across the country? You weren't exiled from the state."

"I thought it would clear my head."

"You can clear it here. Only now, you can see your mom every day. And with you here, I won't have to come back and forth. Plus Joe's in Albany, I'm in Manhattan so there's no chance of you running into one of us."

Yeah, but I see him a lot more often on the news here.

They finally settled on Mark strongly considering the option. Livia apologized for having to take off early. She had gotten a call to go look over newly collected evidence for a high profile case. She told Mark she'd only be able to stick around for another half hour. With that, they finished up and headed right over to the storage facility. This was the part of the day Mark had been dreading the most. The last time he saw this locker was a decade ago and it was a nightmare back then.

The place was only five minutes from the burger joint, and it took them another five to navigate the labyrinth that was its layout. They came upon the right locker and Mark had to dust off the lock before opening it. As he lifted the door, he and Livia coughed as a wave of dust and musty air escaped. When Mark reached for the light and switched it on, they realized it looked better in the dark.

It looked like an episode of Hoarders. There were boxes upon boxes, a lot from Mark's old house as a child. Livia stuck around just long enough to make a mental catalog and come up with a game plan with Mark. He still had to fly back the next day, but she could help out for the rest of the week. They decided that either way, Mark would come back in the following weeks for at least a week. The more he thought about it, the more he realized that moving back home was inevitable.

Livia took her leave and Mark began digging. He knew he wasn't getting anything done tonight; it was more about taking an inventory and seeing what it would take to clean this place out. It certainly wasn't getting done any time soon. Just then a chill shuddered down Mark's spine. It was as if a gust of wind had just come through, despite that fact that he was indoors. The longer he spent in this room, the more he got that strange feeling that he was being watched. *How the hell did that thing follow me here?*

After nearly an hour, he had had enough and left, almost forgetting to lock up. There was something in there and Mark couldn't explain it. He had never heard of Kushtaka ever leaving its natural area; though it wasn't exactly an exact science. Most of the research he read was from so-called experts that claimed to have seen the creature. Either way, he felt better getting out of the storage locker. He and Livia had found the perfect place for his mother and he decided that he would most likely move out of his self-initiated exile. Today was an accomplishment.

TEN

Mark walked into the Capitol Building with his stomach full and the taste of hot roast beef still in his teeth. Due to his newfound financial stability, he was able to eat out for lunch every day and he savored it. As he walked through security, he waved and smiled at the officers whom he saw every day, yet honestly couldn't recall any of their names. Just when he was about to walk towards the elevator, one of the older looking guards stopped him,

"Mr. Thomas asked us to tell you stop by his office when you got back."

"Thanks, tell him I'll be right there."

"Of course. He told me to tell you it was urgent."

Well now, what could that be about? Mark made his way up to Joe's office and the door was wide open. Joe was sitting at his desk working on his computer and had looked like he'd seen better days. Mark wasn't sure what, but something was clearly bothering him. He knocked on the wall as he walked in. Joe looked up and his expression didn't change at all. He flatly said, "Shut that please."

Now slightly alarmed, Mark closed the door and sat down. All at once a rush of thoughts went through Mark's head. *He knows, he must know. How could he know? I hid it perfectly. Only an audit would have revealed it and that would have gone by my desk.*

Maybe that's not it at all. Mark calmed himself down for the moment, realizing that until he knew what was on Joe's mind, there was no point speculating. After what seemed to be an hour, but was only seconds, Joe began to speak:

"Mark, I know what you've been doing?"

Shit, he does *know!*

"Joe, what are you talking about?" chuckled Mark in a desperate attempt to play dumb.

"Cut the shit, Mark! What the hell is the New York Civil Service Retirement Fund?" demanded Joe as he threw an account statement at Mark. He didn't have to guess which account it was.

Mark said nothing. He could already feel himself sweating and his hot roast beef lunch was getting ready to work its way back up his esophagus. *How did he find out? How could he not have? It's not like I did that great a job of hiding it. But how did he know to look there?* The room suddenly became quite hot as Mark's greatest fear was now a reality.

"Well?" asked Joe, still furious.

"I don't know what to say," said Mark, his voice low and shameful.

"Jesus Christ! There's five million dollars in here! What the hell were you thinking?!"

"You want the honest to God truth?"

"Of course I do."

"I made a few bad investments…"

"You dumbass! How the hell do you even let it get that bad?!"

"I don't really have a good answer to that question. How'd you find out?"

"Livia. You really shouldn't try keeping secrets from

her."

That blow hit harder than any insult Joe could have thrown. He always knew that Livia and Joe were close friends, he just never suspected *that* close. What gave them the right to conspire behind his back? They were both traitors. Mark's fear now turned to anger for both his wife and best friend. Joe took notice of Mark's changing face and spoke in a calmer tone:

"Mark, she came to me with this statement, suspicious of what it was for. She asked you about it and told me you practically screamed pathological liar when explaining it."

"Still, you had no right…"

"No right to what…know that my partner and friend is *stealing millions*?! I mean, shit, how much do you owe?"

"Actually, it's paid off."

"What?"

"It's paid…"

"Explain that to me please!"

"I owed nine hundred grand and paid it off five months ago," explained Mark, knowing there was no point in denying it. The survivalist in him came out and knew that his best shot was to cooperate and maybe get a lesser sentence.

"So if you only owed that much, why…?"

"I was desperate, then it was more for convenience."

"Convenience?!"

Joe sat back and actually laughed. Mark knew him well enough to know that it wasn't because he was amused. Oftentimes, when a situation was so screwed up, the only response was to laugh out of not knowing any other way to express the intense emotion. Very quickly, Joe's rage returned and his death glare was fixed on Mark. If ever there was an ideal moment for Mark to have a heart attack and end his miserable life, right then and there would have been it.

The smell of bacon took Mark from his horrible nightmare about the past. It was much earlier than he had woken up yesterday. Ironically, just as he was getting used to Eastern Time again, it was the day he had to fly back. He glanced over into the kitchen and his mother was making bacon and eggs. She smiled at him when she saw he was awake and said, "I thought I'd make us a treat for today."

Mark smiled, genuinely touched and got up to make sure she was operating the stove correctly. They shared a lovely breakfast and his mother was surprisingly lucid. Something told Mark that deep down, she knew everything that had happened with him. At the very least, she knew he was leaving today. At the end of breakfast, she looked right at her son and declared, "No matter what, I'll always love you. You know that right?" Nearly drawn to tears at the poignancy, Mark nodded. He told his mother he loved her and he'd back in three weeks. While he didn't tell her or Livia, he had already made up his mind to move back.

After packing his bags, he thought about calling Livia, then decided not to. That relationship could be repaired, just not now. He knew they'd never be married again, but would settle for civil acquaintances, maybe even friends. With that he was off, and for the first time in a long time, Mark had an optimistic view of his future.

KUSHTAKA

He had promised Livia to at least get a start on the storage locker. Seeing as how he didn't have to be at the airport for another three hours, he figured he could get something done in there. He went in with a brand new box of trash bags and spent two hours filling eight of them. The first wave was just getting actual trash out. These were items that were broken beyond repair, infested with bugs or mold or were just in such a terrible state they belonged in the garbage.

The entire time, Mark was on high alert. That strange feeling he got in there yesterday wasn't back, but he didn't forget about it. As he went through box after box, it was like a treasure trove of childhood memories. He found an old sled from when he was five, his soccer jersey from middle school and a box with every test and report card he ever got. *Mom really saved everything didn't she.*

Just when he was getting ready to finish up and head to the airport, Mark stumbled upon one more box, this one older than many of the others and buried deep in a corner. As he picked it up, he realized it was much heavier than it looked. He grunted and set it down on top of a metal toolbox. Upon opening it, Mark nearly jumped back, half from the cold air that came out and half from seeing what it was.

This particular box contained all of Mark's father's old "trinkets". Mark hadn't seen any of this since before his father died. He pulled out a set of black candles, a Ouija board and the black book he once saw his father reading. Mark could have sworn he saw the book levitating in the air, but it was so long ago, and he had convinced himself it was a dream. At the very least, the book existed, with its gold lettering and strange symbols on the cover. *What were you trying to do Dad?*

Mark dug deeper into the box and found an old composition book, filled with his father's handwriting. As he flipped through the pages, Mark was amazed at what he was holding in his hands. His father died when he was so young that Mark never really got to know him and here was his journal. Finally Mark would have a chance at understanding the man he was and more importantly, what exactly had happened to him.

Checking the time, Mark realized he was supposed to leave for the airport twenty minutes earlier. He had cleaned out a lot for the time he was here and the rest would just have to wait until he came back in a few weeks. Immediately and without hesitation, he took both books with him. The Ouija board and candles were a bit creepy and he was sure that the books would be sufficient for now.

As he got into the car, he slipped the books into his one and only carryon bag. Mark thought about reading the books during the long flight but felt their physical appearance might draw negative attention. *There'll be plenty of time to read it when I get home.* He settled on reading a TIME Magazine he bought at the airport bookstore. Once the plane took off, he opened the magazine and was slightly disturbed to find a spotlight on Joe Thomas along with nine other "Governors to Watch" in a series of articles. *One reconciliation at a time.*

Landing in Alaska was strange, since it was only an hour after he left. He remembered having a hard time adjusting to that when he first moved here. Paul was waiting for him at the airport and they sat down for lunch at a diner across the street. Just like breakfast, Mark offered to pay as thanks for Paul chauffeuring him around. Paul didn't complain.

"So how was Philadelphia," asked Paul, still believing that's where Mark had been.

"It was good, great actually," explained Mark, being honest about how it went.

"Cool. Oh, you probably haven't heard."

"Heard what?" asked Mark, eager to know if any of his Alaska problems had updates.

"Jimmy got attacked, he's fine. But Monday night, something came at him behind the bar. He said it looked like a black bear."

"He's okay though, right?"

"Yeah, he had his rifle and fired off like two or three shots. Craziest thing is, whatever this was, it didn't go down. Jimmy swears one of the shots hit it, but it kept running and the next morning there was no blood anywhere."

Mark sat in stunned silence. He had been gone for just a few days and this Kushtaka was wreaking havoc. What would it do now that he was back? After lunch, Paul dropped Mark off at his cabin. He brought his bag inside and immediately took out the books he got from his father's box. He was most interested in the journal, but there was something almost ethereal to this black book. Its title sounded Latin and it looked like something a witch would use to raise the dead.

For some reason, he was drawn to the black book. He slowly opened the brittle, dusty cover and read the introduction. It was both amusing and incredibly disturbing. The editor of this book claimed that it was written hundreds of years ago in the Middle East. *Well that's how you start a creepy story.* What unsettled Mark was when he noticed in the special thanks section, the editor thanked a specific demon by name. *Was Dad one of these nutcases?*

In one sitting, he read the entire first chapter. And if he thought the introduction was weird, he had no words to describe these pages of text, allegedly written by some desert wanderer centuries ago. The Narrator discussed how he survived in the desert and essentially bragged that he knew ways to summon the "Ancient Ones", which Mark assumed had to be deities, demons or both.

After just a single chapter, Mark put the book down. It wasn't exactly a page turner and it left him with more questions than answers. He wondered if the Kushtaka could be one of these "Ancient Ones" the book mentioned. At first, it was easy to write this all off as foolish superstition, but the more he thought about everything that was happening in town lately, the more he believed that there might be something to all of this.

It was now almost dinner time and Mark decided to head over to McHenry's and check in on Jimmy. He had to admit that his main reason for doing so was hearing the story from Jimmy. This could be a chance to corroborate any evidence that the Kushtaka might be real. If so, it meant that he was not the only target and, unfortunately for Jimmy, that it was probably responsible for Kelly's disappearance. According to what Mark had read, it usually targeted children; and those that went missing were never seen or heard from again.

KUSHTAKA

When Mark's truck pulled into Jimmy's, he saw a large crowd gathered. This was becoming a regular occurrence. Each night Jimmy would serve dinner, and right afterwards, they would scour the town and forests hoping to find something, anything from Kelly. Mark wasn't sure if he'd stick around for the search, given his jet lag, but he'd make an effort. At dinner, Jimmy recounted his story to the crowd, with a twist that left Mark vindicated.

"So that sum'bitch ran up to me, was a bear at least six or seven feet and I shot it three times. One in the head, two in the back as it ran."

"Damn, sounds like bigfoot!" called one of the patrons.

"I think it's the thing that took my Kelly. And if I see it again, its head is going up on that wall!"

The crowd cheered as Jimmy was invigorated and ready to save his daughter by any means necessary. Within an hour, they were outside and on the move. They still had a good two hours before dusk and could get a lot of ground covered. The truth was most of the town had conceded the fact that they believed poor little Kelly was dead or worse. Most continued on because no one had the heart to tell Jimmy they were giving up. Plus it had become some sort of strange bonding experience for everyone in town. Obviously, no one was glad she was missing, but many had grown closer and formed new friendships from the search parties.

Mark decided to call it a night and head back home. He thanked Jimmy and apologized for not being able to stick around longer, but promised he'd be there the next night. Jimmy had no shortage of volunteers to help find Kelly. This of course, was disheartening for another reason. They had a lot of ground to cover, and the fact that so many people were looking for so long and still hadn't found her was not a good sign. No one wanted to admit the brutal truth.

It was now dusk as Mark drove his way back to his cabin. He partly wished he hadn't even gone out now. He could have stayed home and been asleep already.

It didn't matter, he was almost there anyway. As he turned a sharp corner, something leapt out in front of his truck. He slammed on the brakes and tried to turn, but there was no time. The impact hit him like a punch in the chest and his truck spun out of control.

The truck came to a screeching halt and Mark's heart almost pounded out of his chest. Against his better judgment, he got out to survey the damage to his truck. To his astonishment the front was entirely unscathed and there was no blood or any sign of an animal. The longer he thought about it, the more sense it began to make. The Kushtaka was at it again, and this time it nearly killed him. Even if he moved back to Buffalo, he was certain this thing would follow him.

Mark went home and barricaded the cabin. He thought about reading more of the black book or his dad's journal, but was tired beyond recognition. He fought to stay awake long enough to walk into his bedroom and make sure the rifle was still there. Apparently it wouldn't kill the Kushtaka, but like with Jimmy, it might make it run away. He didn't know why, but he was damn sure going to find out.

ELEVEN

Little Mark looked at the clock wishing he knew how to tell time. They hadn't learned that yet in school. He wanted to know how long he had been there but Mrs. Jenkins, the mean old lady that lived next door, wouldn't tell him. Her house smelled funny too. Little Mark just wanted to go home, but the ambulance men told him he had to stay with the neighbor for now. After he called 911, they came and got Mommy. Little Mark asked them when he'd see her again, but they wouldn't tell him. He tried not to be scared, but a part of him thought he might never see her again.

Before dawn Mark was awake and now reading his father's journal. It was amazing how much was in there. Mark had always known that he taught Philosophy at a university, and the ruling theory was that he suffered from schizophrenia and ended his life when the hallucinations became too much to deal with. Reading his dad's journal made Mark understand him in a way he never thought he would.

Mark nearly cried as he went through entries that mentioned him and his mother. For the first time in his life, he saw remorse from his father at devoting so much time and energy to his research instead of his family. Of course, these were only the first few entries. As time went on, they became increasingly more bizarre. His father had developed a fascination, and eventual obsession with the paranormal. He wrote:

Religion has still failed to show any definitive proof on this world or existence beyond our own. They say that blessed are those who believe, but have not seen, but I have no time for such naivety. I must know.

Well wasn't he kind of arrogant?

After an hour, Mark had to put it down. It was a bit much to take in for one sitting and he needed to go to work anyway. He had yet to tell Tim about his plans to move back home and was not looking forward to the conversation. He felt like he hadn't really been there when they needed him most. He hoped Tim would understand, but worried that he may be stuck in that job forever.

Mark headed right for Tim's office to give him the news. Tim look relieved to see him and opened with, "I'm hoping you have an answer for me and it's good news?"

"We need to talk," sighed Mark as he sat down. Tim's expression changed.

"What's it gonna take?"

"It's not about that. I'm moving back. Back home."

"Oh? Is everything all right? I know you said…"

"Yeah, I'm checking my mom into a nursing home, and I think it's time to go back where I belong."

"Can't argue with that. When were you looking to go?"

"Three weeks, maybe a month. Just enough time to get everything together and settled."

"How open would you be to getting paid more for that duration of time? Wouldn't it help you with the move?"

"What do you mean?"

"Look Mark, I'm leaving no matter what, over the weekend. Unless you take this job, this place won't have a manager and the owners may shut it down or bring in someone else. How about this, be the acting manager until you have to leave and it'll buy me time to get someone permanent?"

Mark really didn't want to get any more involved than he already was. But at the same time, he didn't want to leave his coworkers stranded and the extra money would help. Reluctantly, Mark agreed and gave a five weeks limit. After that, whether they had a new manager or not, he would be heading back to Buffalo. Tim thanked him and shook his hand. With no time to waste, Tim had two days to train Mark. Their work was cut out for them the rest of the week.

After a long and arduous day, Mark was finally done. Management was certainly less physically exhausting, but it reminded him of being back in that cubicle counting other people's money. Until he saw the ledgers, he never realized just how much money the owners made off this place, after paying the workers next to nothing. It didn't matter right now though. Mark had bigger fish to fry than corporate greed.

As soon as he left the lumber yard, he headed right

for the hardware shop where Ethan worked. He hadn't seen him since last week and had since done his research on the Kushtaka. Mark wasn't sure what to expect, but was hoping Ethan would lend his expertise on the subject. After all, he's the one who originally brought it up.

Mark walked up to a locked door and a closed sign. This was strange, seeing as how the hours were until eight-thirty and he spotted Ethan's car in the parking lot. He walked around back and heard someone rustling around on the inside. He looked through the window, wondering how creepy he must have looked peering in like a stalker. Ethan was definitely in there, he was walking around packing up boxes. Mark knocked on the window and Ethan jumped. When he saw it was Mark he looked relieved and pointed to the back door.

The door was already open when Mark got there. He walked in and Ethan closed and locked it behind him. Mark took a look around and there were several boxes and bags packed up.

"Ethan, what are you moving?" asked Mark, only half sarcastically.

"Yeah," answered Ethan, not sarcastic at all.

"Look, you were right about the Kus…"

"Don't say it!" shouted Ethan, startling Mark.

"Sorry."

"No, I'm sorry. It's just, the more we discuss it, the more we draw its energy toward us. It's how it chooses its victims."

"Well wait, I need your help. There has to be a way we can get rid of it. Was there anything in the old legends or stories?"

"No, your best bet is to get as far away as possible."

"How far we talking?"

"I've heard stories of it going as far east as Vancouver and south as Seattle. I'm heading to San Francisco. I doubt it'll go that far. I recommend you do the same."

"I can't, I'm actually moving back to Buffalo."

"Good, leave tonight. Trust me, it's the best thing you can do. The amount of attacks, the little girl going missing, it isn't coincidence."

"What are you talking about?"

"It already has one soul, that poor child. It mauled your friend and attacked another one. This creature becomes more and more powerful with every soul it enslaves. They've always been around, but sometimes their activity spikes and they become powerful and dangerous. I believe...I know that time is now. The last time it happened was over a hundred years ago and it lasted a decade before it went dormant again."

"Why just go back if it was so powerful?"

"No one knows. And the moral of every story I heard was to get away from it."

Mark didn't agree with Ethan's plan, but he understood it. He offered to help him pack out of politeness and Ethan declined for the same reason. They shook hands and wished each other well. It was clear that there was no talking Ethan into staying or Mark into leaving immediately. Ethan did leave him with a final parting suggestion, "Whether you decide to stay or leave, don't try and fight it. Just run."

These words resonated in Mark with a lingering foreboding. That was until he was a mile away from the hardware shop. The closer he got to his cabin the more he began to wonder. *What the hell does he know? He's running like a coward. There has to be a way to defeat this bastard.* Mark suddenly felt bad for thinking about his friend this way. He wasn't sure where these thoughts were coming from.

He got home and felt an urge to keep reading his father's journal. Maybe in his vast research and experiments, he came across some information on the Kushtaka. Maybe Mark was *meant* to find that box in the storage locker. The more he thought about it, the more it felt like it had called out to him, begging to be found.

No sooner was Mark through the door, the journal was open right where he left off. Now his father started writing about the mysterious black book Mark had read the first chapter of. At first, the journal was skeptical about its legitimacy. It had been heavily rumored that the book was actually written by a famous author. But as Mark's father conducted more research, he became convinced that this book was real.

The next few entries documented his tireless search to procure this book. He happened upon one at a used bookstore and paid only fifty cents for it. The entry revealed how hilarious Mark's father thought it was that this fool of a clerk had no idea what he was practically giving away. The next entry was a commentary of the first chapters. Like Mark, his father had been thrown off a bit by how odd the first chapter was. But he assured the reader that it got more interesting along the way. It said the book may in fact, hold the secrets to summoning an ancient and awesome power.

Mark then turned his attention to the black book and skimmed over the next few chapters. The journal was right in that this book did contain rituals and recitations to be used when summoning spirits. *Is this where the Kushtaka came from? Maybe somebody used one of these thousands of years ago and unleashed it.* It was a longshot, seeing as how the Kushtaka seemed to only appear in Tlingit and Tsimian folklore. This book was written in Syria centuries before Columbus or Leif Ericson.

That same chill he felt in the storage locker returned to him now. Was this the Kushtaka or something else? Either way, it terrified Mark and he put the book down. Was he in over his head or had he not committed either way? As he slowly backed himself into his bedroom and barricaded the door shut, he grabbed the rifle and climbed into bed. There was one other possible solution to his problem, and he would give that a shot in the morning.

TWELVE

"I'm not having you arrested," explained Joe, less stern and more professional.

"What?" asked Mark, almost out of reflex.

"Don't get me wrong, you're a piece of shit and you deserve to rot in prison. And as much as I'd like to see that happen, it's not in my best interest."

"I don't understand."

"Settle down, the last thing I need is you having a heart attack in here. Here's what's going to happen. You're going to hand over all the information for that phony account so the money can be returned to the state, then you're going to resign for personal reasons."

"I can't just quit, no notice."

"You can, and you will. Make something up if you have to."

"What about Livia?"

"Well, when I talked to her this morning, she said she'll want to have a talk with you too. Christ, you screwed up royally Mark, you really did."

"I'm sorry."

"Don't, just don't. I don't have the time or patience to hear any more of your bullshit. I'm not doing this for you. You and I both know that I've got senators and congressmen that would just love to crucify me and stop me from getting reelected. I'm not about to let them win via some scandal because your stupid ass can't keep his hands out of the piggy bank. Your wife feels the same way. Neither of us want an embarrassment like you dragging us down."

That last bit really stung. Mark had worked hard his entire life to make something of himself and he couldn't fathom that one little mistake could unravel it all. He knew he was done politically. Joe Thomas promised him that if he so much as ran for a school board, he'd have him arrested and use his own wife to prosecute him to the fullest. Life, at least as Mark had known it, was over now.

He wasn't even allowed back into his office. Livia would come by later and clear it out. Joe had given him a day to draft his resignation letter and make it sound believable. The worst sting of all, however, came when Mark got home. When he got inside, Livia was nowhere to be found. Mark found a note from her on the inside of the front door which read, "Staying in Manhattan for the week. Pack your things and leave." It was at that point that Mark knew he simply couldn't go on here. If he ever wanted a normal life again, he'd have to crawl into some corner on the other side of the world.

A loud howling woke up Mark before six. He didn't have to guess what it was. The Kushtaka somehow knew he was onto it. As soon as he was up, he called Tim and left a message that he'd be a little late. *What's he gonna do, fire me?* According to Ethan, there was no tried and true method of expelling the Kushtaka, at least not for the Tlingit people. Once it had built up its momentum, there was no stopping it. *There's one other person who might help me.*

He looked up the phone number to the church rectory and dialed it, but only got the answering machine. It was still pretty early and Mark figured even priests slept in sometimes. It didn't matter, he was getting an answer no matter what. After a hearty breakfast, Mark hopped into his truck and headed right over to the church.

Each door was locked and there didn't appear to be anyone there. After waiting around for twenty minutes, he spotted Father Hauser opening up the doors to the church and walking in with a few candles. He followed while trying not to look shady. As he got into the doorway he called out, "Father Hauser!" Hauser turned around and Mark recoiled upon seeing his face. The normally handsome priest had boils on his face and they looked painful.

"That bad huh?" Hauser asked, reading Mark's expression.

"My God. What happened?"

"Couldn't tell you. They just sprang up."

"When?"

"Actually it was the day after I blessed your house."

Mark's heart sank. Had he been responsible for this? He had never heard of the Kushtaka causing boils; that sounded more biblical than anything else. But there was no denying that something evil had its eye on Mark and probably didn't like Father Hauser coming into the situation.

"I'm sorry," apologized Mark.

"Don't be. Mark, I'm glad you're here actually. I've been meaning to talk to you."

"Okay."

"You need to leave that house."

"It's not the house that's evil Father, it's something else."

"What do you know about it?" asked Hauser, slightly suspicious.

Mark went on to explain everything he knew about the Kushtaka. He told Hauser about the connection with Kelly missing, Barry getting mauled and Ethan leaving town. Hauser had to sit down to take it all in.

"You're suggesting the existence of this, Alaskan mythological creature?"

"Myths are often based on some reality. This thing attacked me in my car, I know I felt the impact and my car was dent free and there was no sign of the large animal that hit it. How do you explain that?"

"I can't. I can't explain any of this. I don't know what's in your house or why it lashed out at me. All I know is that your best option is to pray and ask God for help."

"Where did that get you? Look at your face," said Mark, regretting it at the last second.

Hauser just shook his head. "Look, my advice is, get out of the house, start praying and I can talk to the archbishop about conducting an investigation."

"An investigation? How long does that take?"

"I don't know, it's really not my specialty. Maybe a few weeks?"

"I don't have that much time. What about performing an exorcism on the premises?"

"Out of the question."

"Why?"

"There's a million bureaucratic loopholes you need to

go through to do that. Now, I'm more than willing to help you out. But you have to do it our way. I know it can be frustrating, but we must be patient and trust in God."

"Not when this thing is days or hours away from killing me."

"I'll talk to the archbishop. Please don't do anything rash. If you need a place to stay, you're welcome here. We have a few extra rooms."

"No thanks," snapped Mark as he stormed out.

"Please Mark, remember only God can help you!" Hauser called to Mark as he left the church.

Who the hell did Hauser think he was? Mark may have never heard of a Kushtaka, but growing up Catholic he had heard a thing or two about exorcism and deliverance. Convinced that it was his only other option, he couldn't understand why Hauser wasn't willing to bend a rule or two to help him. *Damn church politics! They'll spend days debating this and meanwhile this thing will take me like it did Kelly!*

Mark got to work pissed off and Tim noticed. It was pretty hard not to. He just figured Mark still didn't really want the job, but Tim was forever leaving Alaska the next morning so at this point, he didn't really care. His only task was showing Mark around again and leaving him the keys at the end of the day.

They went through the day and it was pretty routine. Both men said very little to each other as they each had much more on their minds to worry about. Tim did mention that Barry had been moved to long term care facility. For a few moments, Mark stopped acting like an asshole and seemed genuinely interested in Barry's condition. Tim explained that he was still in the coma and the doctors were saying he had about a one in three chance of waking up.

They reached the end of the day, Tim handed Mark the keys and both went their separate ways. Mark knew he should probably go to the office and start setting it up for himself, but wanted to get right home. There was something waiting for him. On his way out he ran into Paul.

"So, do I call you boss yet?" he asked.

"Not till Monday."

"Oh hey, where were you last night during the search party. Jimmy was asking about you."

"I was busy."

"Oh…okay. Are you coming tonight? A bunch of us are."

"Does nobody understand that the kid is dead already?!" shouted Mark and gaining the attention of at least fifteen other guys heading to their cars. They all stared in shock.

"Now, I didn't mean it like that," Mark explained, now backtracking.

"Look, I know it's tough, but we can't lose our heads. I'll tell him you're sick."

Mark nodded and shamefully went to his car in front of his new subordinates whom he had completely pissed off right before becoming their boss. *That'll make things interesting come Monday, assuming the Kushtaka doesn't kill me by then.* He headed straight home and opened up his father's journal, anxious to see what he had written next.

As Mark delved deep into his obsession, he discovered that his father had progressed from simply researching the paranormal to trying to prove its existence. He did this by collecting Ouija Boards, black candles and had begun regularly using them to contact the dead. He seemed determined, if for no other reason, than to know for sure what truly existed in this world or the next.

Each time his father's journal referenced the black book; Mark would turn to it and read the passage for himself. His father had started to believe in the power of using spirits to benefit himself. Mark did remember that their old house was huge and really nice before his father died. Here was the spell that caused it. Mark's father had found a way to tap into the spiritual world to benefit him. Mark wasn't sure how he felt about this, until he found a passage that intrigued him:

Most ordinary people think demons and devils are one in the same, but I have found the distinction, the difference between them. I have learned what many only dream of knowing. It seems that a demon is nothing but a foot-soldier while the devils are the generals. Like everyone I had always thought of the devil meaning Satan but there are others. Others whose names I dare not write...not in this book at least. Devils are far more powerful than demons or any spirit from other mythologies and folklores.

104

KUSHTAKA

That was the first time that Mark found a reference to "other mythologies" in his father's journal. He wondered what he could have meant by that. In his Kushtaka research, Mark had come across the names of other malevolent spirits from different cultures. The Dybbuk and Wendigo had struck him as particularly disturbing, in addition to the Kushtaka of course.

This got Mark thinking though. The more he read, he found that his father believed that it was possible to summon not only a demon, but one of the devils to do one's bidding. He thought back to that night he swore he saw the black book levitating in the air. *What kind of abilities did Dad get from this? Would it help defeat the Kushtaka?*

Mark thought back to what Ethan and Hauser had both advised him to do. He certainly wasn't interested in running like a coward. That was the old Mark. The Mark that ran to the other side of the country when he screwed up. The Mark that didn't have the courage to stand and fight. That Mark was dead and a new, courageous one stood in his place. *Whatever I have to do to beat this thing, I will*, he promised to himself, prepared for anything.

Father Hauser's advice came to mind now. What about turning to the church? Or at least turning to prayer? That idea was shot down in his mind almost immediately. *Mom said she always prayed for his father and look where that got both of them.* God worked too slowly and Mark needed immediate salvation. He was left with an urgent feeling that the clock was running out and the Kushtaka was moving in for the kill. But what could bring down such a powerful entity? *Sometimes, you have to fight fire with fire.*

For the next few hours, Mark delved even further into his own madness. His father's journal had cataloged several of these demons and devils, along with their specialties and most importantly, the ritual for summoning them. As he read, one name piqued his interest more than the others. In fact, he was almost certain he had heard this name somewhere before. It was called Belial. According to the research, it was a powerful devil, second only to Satan himself. Maybe this was his answer.

The clock in his living room struck midnight with a loud, echoing chime. Mark walked into the other room just to see what the sound was. In the six months he had lived there, he had never heard the clock make a noise like that. He examined it for a minute, confused, and then went back into his bedroom. *I'll sleep on it; figure it out in the morning.*

THIRTEEN

Little Mark waited anxiously at the door. The last four days had been terrible staying with Mrs. Jenkins. She was mean and her macaroni and cheese tasted gross, not like when Mommy made it. He asked Mrs. Jenkins for the millionth time, "What time is Mommy coming?" And for the millionth time Mrs. Jenkins snarled her wrinkled face and answered, "You children need to be more patient."

Finally, Mommy walked in the door and little Mark ran up to her and hugged her for five whole Mississippi's. He never wanted to be away from her again. She took him home next door and sat him down on the couch. She put her hand on little Mark's shoulder and said in her soft voice, "There's something I want to talk to you about."

"What is it Mommy?"

"Mark, I'm really sorry that you found me like that. I know you must have been really scared."

"I was. And I had to stay with Mrs. Jenkins, she's gross and…"

"She was very nice for letting you stay there."

"What happened to you Mommy? How come you wouldn't wake up? I asked everyone, but they wouldn't tell me."

"Mark, Mommy was sick and she had an accident."

"Like Daddy?"

"Kind of, except Mommy is still here. And I promise you, I'm never leaving you again like that. Daddy didn't make it, but from now on *I* will. I love you Mark."

"I love you too Mommy."

The sound of a grown man screaming bellowed through the forest and startled Mark out his sound sleep. As he jumped up and opened his eyes, he could see that it was already daylight. *Must have slept in. What the hell was*...just then, the scream echoed again. Mark quickly threw on his boots, grabbed the rifle and ran outside.

He didn't have to go far, maybe thirty yards into the trees to find another sight of horror. There, leaning up against a tree was a severed leg, which stopped at the kneecap. Mark took one look at this, especially the boot on the leg and knew right away it was Barry's. *It's taunting me!* He stepped back from the disfigured limb and shouted, "What the hell do you want with me?!" There was no answer, but the bloody leg made the message pretty clear.

That was it. No more games, no more putting off. Mark knew exactly what he had to do. He wasn't crazy about this idea, but it was all he had left. The Kushtaka's message to him was loud and clear. When Mark got back in the house, he went right to his father's journal and reread everything he could about Belial. According to his father's research, this particular devil despised all others. *The enemy of my enemy is my friend.*

Immediately, he went to the black book and

compared the notes to his father's journal, specifically on the subject of summoning. Mark stopped in surprise when he came across the suggestion to use an animal sacrifice. These books argued that only through an offering of flesh and blood would these spirits be prepared to do your bidding. While this disturbed Mark intently, desperation often brought out the worst in people.

Mark had a hard time wrapping his head around this idea as he pulled into the only pet shop in town. *Am I seriously doing this?* He took a deep breath and walked inside. A friendly and cute brunette greeted him with, "Good afternoon, can I help you with anything?" Mark simply shook his head and told her he was just looking. She looked him up and down and decided to keep an extra eye on him. Mark figured he must have looked like the epitome of creepy right now.

He looked up and down the cages and pens; they had puppies, kittens, rabbits, guinea pigs and a few ferrets. Glancing over to the other side of the shop he saw an array of fish. *I don't suppose a fish would work for this?* Everything he'd heard or read about this, it was usually a chicken or a cow or a small mammal. While this place didn't have the first two, it definitely had the latter.

Just then, the bell chimed as another customer walked in. It was a little girl and her dad. They walked up to the counter and the father said he was just there to pick up some more rabbit food. The friendly clerk walked over and grabbed a few bags of it for him. The little girl ran over to the rabbits' pen right next to Mark. She peered inside and called,

"Daddy, can we get another bunny?"

"No honey, one's enough for now," he answered, handing the clerk money for the food.

"But Winston needs a friend," she pleaded.

What kind of kid names a rabbit Winston?

"You take care of him for a few more months and we'll talk. Okay?"

"Okay, fine."

She ran back to her father who gave Mark a polite nod and smile. Mark looked at the rabbits that little girl wanted. He hated himself for it, but his mind was already made up. There was no way he could bring himself to sacrifice one of the dogs or cats, he had grown up with them. But fortunately for him, he had never had a rabbit as a pet. It would serve his purposes well. There were six of them playfully running around the pen, and Mark was having trouble deciding which one's life would come to an abrupt end later that day.

The clerk rang him up and he carried the poor, unsuspecting animal out in a little cardboard box with holes. When he got home, he set the box down and didn't want to look at it or think about it until it was time. *I'm going to hell for this aren't I?* On his way home, he had stopped for a few other items and took them out of their bags. He had chalk and a set of black candles. He had everything he needed, except for the foresight to know if this insane plan would actually work.

It was now almost dusk and everything was in its place. Mark had drawn a pentagram on the floor in chalk and surrounded it with the lit black candles. Its diameter was almost ten feet. The cardboard box containing the unfortunate rabbit was next to it. Mark sat down in the center with the black book, ready to begin.

Mark recited an opening incantation in a language he didn't understand. It wasn't even Latin, and he was sure he was butchering the pronunciation. He couldn't help but feel ridiculous. Next, he moved to the main event. He picked up the long, sharpened steak knife which sat next to the box. He then removed the lid and pulled out the rabbit with his other hand. It squirmed and moved its legs trying to get its bearings. *I'm sorry little guy, but it's me or you.*

He placed the rabbit down in the center of the pentagram, trying to be gentle. As he took the knife and brought it up to the little thing's neck, he said aloud, "This pact I seal with blood." With one quick jerk, he slit its throat and spilled the blood on the ancient symbol. Turning to the proper page, he recited the summoning spell specific to Belial. There was a version in English, as well as, what appeared to be Arabic. Despite his lack of linguistic skills, he went with Arabic, thinking it was somehow more mystical that way.

When he was finished, he closed the book, not sure what to expect now. After a few seconds of silence a gust of cold air blew through the room and extinguished the candles. Mark took this as a sign of success. *What the hell did I just do?* Slightly ashamed of performing the ritual, Mark quickly threw out the candles, the dead rabbit and the box. He then cleaned up the blood and chalk off the floor. Within a half hour, there was no sign of it at all.

Night began to fall and Mark was getting nervous.

How would he know that it worked? As a precaution, he ate dinner with Jimmy's rifle beside him. He honestly meant to return it, eventually, probably when he moved back to Buffalo. The wind began to howl and Mark jumped up, anticipating something else. He wasn't sure exactly how this process would work. Would the Kushtaka simply never appear again, or would it make one final stand?

It wasn't long before Mark's question was answered. A voice called out from the darkness, like it had so many times before. "Mark!" it yelled. Upon hearing the voice, Mark was astonished to hear that it was Livia's this time. *What do you take me for?* He got up and headed for the door, rifle in hand. As he opened it, he saw Livia standing at the edge of the front yard, wearing the same outfit from the last time he saw her.

"Mark, can I come in? I'm sorry for everything."

"What are you doing here?" asked Mark, caught off guard.

"I thought we could talk. Make up for everything."

As much as he wanted it to be true, he fought the urge to give in and shouted, "Go back to the hole you crawled out of!"

With that, Mark turned to go back inside and shut the door, when he now heard a ferocious growl. He turned back and now the Kushtaka had left Livia's form and taken one of a massive black bear. Out of reflex, Mark pointed his rifle at it and backed up into the house. The Kushtaka charged with all the speed and savagery of the bear it resembled.

Mark had only just gotten himself into the house when the beast was already on the front porch. He reached for the trigger when the creature stopped in mid-air, as if struck by an unseen wall. It was then hurled backwards, and hit the ground kicking up dirt and dust from the impact. Mark's front door then slammed shut by itself. What followed next what the most horrific event Mark had ever witnessed, and he didn't even see any of it.

What he assumed must have been the Kushtaka still in bear form, let out an unnerving cry. It wasn't one of anger or viciousness, but of fear and pain. Mark heard thump after thump and could feel the vibrations caused by each. *Is it being thrown like a ragdoll?* The beast then let out a sound that was long and agonizing to listen to. It sounded like a wolf, then a cat, followed by a bear, a dog, and a half dozen other animal sounds that Mark didn't recognize.

There was no doubt in Mark's mind; this had to be Belial at work. And it wasn't just killing the Kushtaka, it was toying with it. Mark had no idea how he knew this, but he got a strong feeling that this devil enjoyed watching the Kushtaka suffer. There was one final loud boom which resulted in the entire cabin shaking to its core. Mark had to hold on to a wall to avoid falling on the floor. After that, there was nothing but silence.

Mark sat by the front door for about an hour, not sure whether or not to open it and look outside. Something told him he didn't want to do that, at least not till morning. He went into his bedroom and crawled into bed. Even though there were a million things racing through his mind, he tried to fall asleep. He gripped the rifle close and hoped his ordeal was finally over.

FOURTEEN

For the first time in two weeks, Mark woke up feeling peaceful. There had been no nightmares from his past, no trouble sleeping and no ominous feeling that something was stalking him. He didn't want to think too soon, but maybe his hell was finally over. *After last night, it* better *be over.* The thought of that reminded him to check outside. Ever cautious, he grabbed the rifle and slowly opened his front door.

In an action hero fashion, Mark leapt over the threshold and swung the rifle in all directions. After seeing no immediate threat and realizing how ridiculous he must have looked, Mark lowered the rifle and walked out onto the front yard. About fifteen feet from the front door it sat; a sight that was both grotesque yet immensely relieving.

On the ground lay a sea otter as lifeless as the poor rabbit he had sacrificed the night before. As Mark stepped in closer, he noticed that the devil was sending him a message. The otter had its throat cut open and a pentagram was carved into its chest. Mark reached over with the rifle and poked it to ensure it was in fact dead. As soon as the edge of the metal chamber touched it, the otter's corpse disintegrated into dust, right before Mark's eyes. Surely the Kushtaka had no true physical form it could revert to in death, but this was Mark's way of knowing it was over. *Message received, thanks.*

Mark went back inside and actually enjoyed his breakfast. When he was finished, he got the sudden urge to call Livia and see how things were going. He also wanted to alert her as to what he was doing in Alaska and when he was moving permanently back to Buffalo. Unlike before, there was no dreading or hesitation when dialing her number. This time, he even had butterflies in his stomach, the good kind. "Hello? Mark?" answered Livia, surprised, but not annoyed.

"Hey Liv, how's it going?" asked Mark, laid back and happy.

"Great, long time no see, huh? Listen, I wanted to thank you for getting started with the storage locker. I'm heading back there next week and I'll…"

"Don't even worry about it. I'm gonna tackle it when I come back."

"You're going to clean out that whole place in just a week?"

"No, I uh…I took your advice. I'm getting things settled here and moving back home."

"Really? That's great. It'll be good for you and your mom. When are you coming?"

"Probably about a month or month and a half. But I'll be there. I actually just finally solved the big problem I had here."

"That's great. I have to run, but it was great catching up and I'm looking forward to you being back here. I'll even help you move if you want."

"I hold you to it."

He ended the call with a wide smile on his face.

Mark then turned his attention to his list of things to do today. He had to start clearing out the cabin. Fortunately, he hadn't brought much and most of the crap inside was already here when he moved in, so he didn't need to take it with him. He needed to stop by the lumber mill and make sure things were good to go for his first day as manager tomorrow and he wanted to check in on Barry. He wasn't sure why, but a small part of him thought that, since the Kushtaka was dead or gone or whatever it was, maybe Barry could start to recover now.

Looking around the house, Mark immediately decided that cleaning up and packing could wait. He had at least five weeks, and most likely wouldn't even start until he only had a few days left. With that, he got in his truck and was off. On his way through town, he drove by the church and noticed it crowded for service. Not quite as much as last week, but still probably a lot more than they were used to. Had Mark not been so pissed at Father Hauser, he would probably be there too. He still felt bad for Jimmy though. A small part of him had wondered if Kelly would come back after the creature died. When she didn't, Mark figured it was never going to happen. That was just something Mark would have to live with, along with everything else.

Stopping at the lumber mill didn't take long at all. He made sure his keys worked and all the papers and schedules were in order for the week. Tim had done a great job of leaving Mark set up for the next few weeks. His goal was to move back to Buffalo before having to do any of it himself. That gave him about four weeks by the looks the paperwork Tim left behind. Mark did one more sweep of his new office to make sure it was good to go and then he was off again.

As he pulled up to the nursing home that Barry was now staying in, it reminded him of the one his mother was soon to be living in. It had that quaint and cozy feel to it. He entered the "coma" wing. The nurse called it something else, but he had never heard that word before. He simply knew it as the wing for people that had yet to wake up from prolonged naps. He walked across a row of coma patients, slightly disturbed that they were all together in this large room. Then again, they probably didn't have the resources and these people didn't need privacy.

He finally came upon Barry, pulled up a chair and sat down in it. He looked less freaky than he had at the hospital with all the tubes and massive bandages. He still had a few small ones on him, but according to the doctors, he had been stabilized. He sure didn't look stable though, at least not in the terms of living a normal life. Mark leaned over and said to him, "Barry man, you gotta wake up. I can't do your job forever. Listen, I move back to Buffalo in four weeks, and I really need you to awake by then." Mark chuckled, but didn't feel that he was being disrespectful because he knew Barry was probably laughing on the inside too. He had heard that coma patients can often hear what's going on around them.

"You're welcome," croaked a voice that Mark couldn't believe was coming from Barry. He looked down and Barry was awake with a grin on his face. But as Mark looked into his eyes, he knew this wasn't Barry at all. Its eyes were intense, hypnotic and evil. Its voice was deep and raspy like a chain smoker that had vomited up raw eggs. Mark recoiled with fear, but something told him that there was a familiarity with whatever this was.

"Belial?" asked Mark, out of instinct.

"Good to finally meet you," it laughed followed by a deep cough. It continued, "You know, you really ought to just smother your friend here and put him out of his misery now. This asshole's never waking up."

"What are you doing here?"

"That's it? I save your ass from that bottom dwelling maggot and you don't even have the decency to thank me?"

Mark didn't know what to say. He was simultaneously intrigued, shocked and terrified.

"Surprised to see me?"

"I'm not," answered Mark, finally finding the courage to speak, "There's something I have to know. It's about…"

"Your daddy?"

"How did he really die?"

"You know how. He played a game of hangman with a bed sheet. That dumb bastard sat there choking and gasping for five minutes," it explained, now laughing with a sinister satisfaction.

"What do you want?"

"The hell do you think? What do you think happens when you call on me? I did you a favor, now you do me one. Oh, Little Mark, you were always mine. Why do you think the Kushtaka came so close to getting you all those times, but never did? Why do you think you knew exactly which box to look in for your daddy's books? I've had you marked your entire life! That's right, Daddy offered you up a long time ago, and look where it got that dumb bastard!"

Mark thought back and realized that the presence he felt in this room right now, he had felt before. All those nights he lay in bed, freezing and terrified, this thing had been there with him. It wasn't the Kushtaka that killed his father or covered Hauser's face with boils. Those acts had Belial written all over them. *God, I'm sorry. I never should have…*

"God can't save you!" it shouted, startling Mark now realizing it could hear his thoughts.

"I gave you an offering," argued Mark, desperate.

"That stupid little rodent? Hardly an appetizer," it said with a smile.

"Get ready to drown in holy water. I'll get the pope himself to come down here and exorcise your ass!"

"Go ahead, I dare you!"

Mark had to fight the urge to punch this thing in the face, but remembered it was Barry's body. He stormed off, and as he approached the door, it let out one last provocation, "Enjoy your last night on earth!" He slammed the door shut behind him, and when he got outside, he fell to his knees and clutched his chest. Was this what a panic attack felt like? Was this Belial trying to kill him? He stood back up and realized that this devil kept its word. It wouldn't come for him until tonight. Mark remembered that his father's journal described these spirits as being quite theatrical.

As Mark drove through town, a rush of thoughts and emotions hit him like a speeding train. *What the hell did you do to me Dad?* Mark didn't want to believe that his own father had offered him up years earlier, but it made sense. There were so many close calls when the Kushtaka could have taken him but didn't, yet it took Kelly with ease. If only she had had a demonic protector that was only saving her for itself later.

He nearly crashed his truck when, in the rearview mirror, he spotted something on his forehead. There was no mistaking the pentagram symbol, much like the one on the dead otter, now etched on his own face. Surely, this was Belial's way of marking him and not letting him forget. Mark turned the truck and headed for a place he never thought he'd go to today: the church.

The crowd was mostly gone when he arrived and he leapt out of his truck and ran up to the closed doors. Mark pounded on them and shouted like a madman, "Father Hauser! I need your help!" Within a minute the door opened and Hauser stood on the other end. Mark was astonished to see that his face was now completely clean and boil-free. *It's not targeting him anymore, it's focusing all its energy on me!*

"Mark, are you all right?" asked Hauser with an urgency and concern.

"I need your help."

"Please, come in."

As Mark stepped over the threshold into the church, a violent nausea hit his stomach and he almost threw up on the spot. *It's already starting!* He shook his head and backed up outside and said, "I'd rather we speak out here." Hauser gave Mark a puzzled look, but obliged and stepped outside.

"Is there someone you'd like me call?" he asked, hoping Mark had not done anything drastic.

"How long would it take to get an exorcism performed?"

"Mark, what have you done?" asked Hauser, frustrated, but still concerned.

"I made a mistake and now I'm in over my head. I know. I screwed up, okay! I admit that. But, what I need right now is your help."

"How can I help?"

"I need *something*, anything you could do. Please, I'm desperate."

"I'm not authorized to do an exorcism, hell I'm not even trained for it. The most I could do is bless the house again, and maybe hold mass in it."

"That's it?!"

"I'm sorry Mark. I can notify the archbishop and we can conduct an investigation and take it from there, but you know that it'll take time. There is no magic overnight solution, that's not how God works."

Yeah, that's why I couldn't trust him to handle my problem in the first place!

Mark wasn't satisfied, this wasn't nearly enough. Hauser had already blessed the house and that did nothing! They finally settled on Hauser giving Mark holy water and a crucifix. Again, he urged Mark not to do anything rash and that he would contact the archbishop immediately. Hauser wished him well and hoped that this desperate man would heed his advice. Mark was glad to have accomplished *something*, even if it wasn't everything he wanted.

The second Mark burst through his door; he went right for the fireplace and started a fire. He threw in a few logs that had been sitting next to it all winter. Once the fire was going, he ran into the other room and grabbed the black book and his father's journal. *Dear God, what have I done?* He threw the black book into the fire first and half expected it not to burn at all. As he watched the pages come apart and begin to char, he was glad to be wrong. Mark stared at his father's journal for almost a minute, not sure what to do. That other book had been nothing but disaster, but this one was still the only piece of his father that he had left. The more he thought about it though, the more he realized that it had unfortunately been tainted the same way the other book had. Averting his eyes so as not to watch, he tossed his father's journal into the fire.

Glancing outside, Mark saw that the sun was setting and was overwhelmed with a grim foreboding. In one hand he picked up the crucifix that Father Hauser gave him, and in the other, the aspergillum filled with holy water. He walked from room to room sprinkling the holy water and waving the crucifix. He spoke loudly and firmly, "Belial, you are not welcome here! I command you to leave!"

Mark wasn't even sure what he was saying, honestly he was just reciting what he remembered from a few horror films. There didn't seem to be much of a response at all. He had finished all the rooms and came to his front door. He wasn't sure why this idea was in his head, but the thought of throwing holy water on his front door would prevent it from getting in. He sprinkled it on and shouted, "Belial, you will not enter this house!"

Before he even finished saying the last word, three booming knocks came at the front door. Mark jumped back a foot and had to keep himself composed. After what he had been through, he was prepared for anything. He looked out the window and saw nothing. Then again, he wasn't really expecting to SEE it. Three more knocks came at the wall next to him, followed by three more from his bedroom.

"Get out of here!" he shouted, waving the crucifix.

Three more knocks, this time louder and coming from the roof.

"In the name of Jesus Christ, I command you to leave this place! You are not welcome here!"

The knocks stopped and Mark was cautiously optimistic. *Was that it? Is it over?* Seconds later, Mark received his answer when every single window in every room shattered simultaneously. Mark nearly screamed in terror at the sight and sound of it. He looked at the broken glass on the floor in the kitchen. It looked like something had been thrown in through the window like a rock, but there was no such object; just the remnants of the window. *Nice trick. That all you got?*

"Mark, how could you screw me over like this, we were supposed to be friends," called Joe Thomas. *What? Where did that come from?* With no point of origin, Mark deduced it was in his head.

"She's *your* mother, and you just abandoned her like that," accused Livia, also only in his head.

"Shut up!" Mark shouted into the air, hoping that Belial could hear him.

Mark became more violent with throwing the holy water until there was none left. He then continued to swing the crucifix back and forth shouting, "God commands you to leave!" An unseen force pulled the crucifix from his hand and threw it across the room until it hit the wall. Mark watched in horror as it became embedded in the wood. Joe Thomas' voice came back this time repeating, "You piece of shit, you deserve to rot!" over and over.

It's trying to get in my head, can't let it. Mark ran into his bedroom and picked up the rifle. He wasn't really sure what it would do, but he felt better having it. He heard a loud crash come from the living room and ran over to find the large and heavy bookshelf on the floor with several pieces broken off. He went over to the wall where the crucifix was stuck and as he reached for it, he heard a voice that he hadn't heard in years. "I'm sorry Mark. I'm sorry I put you through all this!" it called. *Dad?*

It didn't sound like it was in his head this time; it actually was coming from the kitchen. He walked over and next to the stove he saw his father, clear as day. He was dressed in a straightjacket and had a bed sheet draped over his shoulder. Mark looked into his eyes and saw a wild and mad intensity about him. *Is this really his spirit or just another hallucination?* "Little Mark, I'm as real as you are," it answered soothingly, somehow knowing what Mark was thinking.

"Dad, what happened?"

"Should never have got involved with these people Little Mark. You know that?"

"Dad what do I do?"

"Nothing son, I'm sorry, your soul's already his. I promised it to him years ago."

Mark still had no idea how much truth was in this. Belial seemed to enjoy torturing the Kushtaka; maybe it was just doing the same thing here. But still, those *were* his father's books and for all Mark knew, he had summoned this devil years ago. It explained why it was following him his entire life and why the Kushtaka never got far with him. *You bastard! How could you do that to your only son?*

"You know how it is Mark, they always make you promise your first born," his 'father' stated matter-of-factly, once again reading Mark's mind.

"I was your son. Didn't that mean anything to you?"

"Of course it did. It helped me find out the truth. They *do* exist, and I have proof now!"

With that, Mark's 'father' began to laugh hysterically. Whether this was a repressed memory, paranormal experience or hallucination, it was now getting to Mark. The only reason he took those books was to better understand his father and he came to realize that the man was nothing but despicable. Either way, he still invited this spirit into Mark's life when he was just a child and he took the coward's way out, instead of being there for his wife and son. *I'd even kill him right now if I could.*

"Go ahead Mark, it'll be fun," he said with a wicked smile, "try and kill me. It'll be like a game!"

Mark lunged forward with the butt of the rifle and savagely attacked this ghostly figure. After a few seconds, his 'father' was gone and Mark realized that all he had done was tear up the stove and leave it filled with dents and holes. *Was that the best you got?* A loud gust of cold wind blew its way through the house. The kitchen table levitated into the air on its own and reached a height of two feet before violently crashing down. Mark ran into the living room when he heard the three knocks. *So we're back to that again?*

Just then, he smelled something funny. *What is that? Smells like...gas!* He glanced over and realized that the fire was still burning in the fireplace and the smell of gas was coming from the kitchen. *Oh my God, the stove!* Mark realized that when he attacked it, he must have punctured the gas line. In a split second, he ran into the kitchen, hoping that his mistake wasn't caught too late, but the fact that he smelled the gas in the living room near the fireplace was a bad sign. Mark lunged toward the front door in an attempt to get out of the cabin before the inevitable happened. *Belial, you clever bastard!*

Just as his hand reached the doorknob, the gas from the stove had finally reached the timid flames and made them furious. The explosion rocked its way from the living room into the kitchen and shot the walls out in every which direction. Mark was immediately struck, not by a wall but by the flames themselves, igniting him into a grotesque inferno. Mark didn't know that anything on earth could be this painful. The fire engulfed him completely, burning holes in his skin and flesh and filling up his lungs with smoke. Unbeknownst to him, the worst was only just beginning. Mark Pallano burned forever, never quite knowing the precise moment when life ended and hell began.